W9-AAB-795

tinkers

tinkers

Paul Harding

BELLEVUE LITERARY PRESS

NEW YORK

First published in the United States in 2009 by
Bellevue Literary Press, New York

FOR INFORMATION ADDRESS:
Bellevue Literary Press
NYU School of Medicine
550 First Avenue
OBV 640
New York, NY 10016

This book was published with the generous support of
Bellevue Literary Press's founding donor the Arnold Simon Family Trust,
the Bernard & Irene Schwartz Foundation
and the Lucius N. Littauer Foundation.

The author wishes to thank the Fine Arts Work Center in Provincetown,
Massachusetts for support during the writing of this book.

Library of Congress Cataloging-in-Publication Data
Harding, Paul, 1967-
Tinkers / Paul Harding. — 1st ed.
p. cm.
1. Reminiscing in old age—Fiction. 2. Identity (Psychology)
in old age—Fiction. 3. Dementia—Patients—Fiction.
4. Psychological fiction. I. Title.
PS3608.A72535T56 2008   813'.6—dc22   2008039887

Book design and type formatting by Bernard Schleifer
Manufactured in the United States of America
ISBN 978-1-934137-12-3 pbk
ISBN 978-1-934137-19-2 hc

5 7 9 8 6

For Meg, Samuel, and Benjamin

1

GEORGE WASHINGTON CROSBY BEGAN TO hallucinate eight days before he died. From the rented hospital bed, placed in the middle of his own living room, he saw insects running in and out of imaginary cracks in the ceiling plaster. The panes in the windows, once snugly pointed and glazed, stood loose in their sashes. The next stiff breeze would topple them all and they would flop onto the heads of his family, who sat on the couch and the love seat and the kitchen chairs his wife had brought in to accommodate everyone. The torrent of panes would drive everyone from the room, his grandchildren in from Kansas and Atlanta and Seattle, his sister in from Florida, and he would be marooned on his bed in a moat of shattered glass. Pollen and sparrows, rain and the intrepid squirrels he had spent half of his life keeping out of the bird feeders would breach the house.

He had built the house himself—poured the foundation, raised the frame, joined the pipes, run the wires, plastered the walls, and painted the rooms. Lightning struck once when he was in the open foundation, soldering the last joint of the hot-water tank. It threw him to the opposite wall. He got up and finished the joint. Cracks in his plaster did not stay cracks; clogged pipes got routed; peeling clapboard got scraped and slathered with a new coat of paint.

Get some plaster, he said, propped up in the bed, which looked odd and institutional among the Persian rugs and Colonial furniture and dozens of antique clocks. Get some plaster. Jesus, some plaster and some wires and a couple of hooks. You'd be all set for about five bucks.

Yes, Gramp, they said.

Yes, Dad. A breeze blew through the open window behind him and cleared exhausted heads. Bocce balls clicked out on the lawn.

Noon found him momentarily alone, while the family prepared lunch in the kitchen. The cracks in the ceiling widened into gaps. The locked wheels of his bed sank into new fault lines opening in the oak floor beneath the rug. At any moment, the floor was going to give. His useless stomach would jump in his chest as if he were on a ride at the Topsfield Fair and with a spine-snapping jolt he and the bed would land in the basement, on top of the crushed ruins of his workshop. George imagined what he would see, as if the collapse had, in fact, already happened: the living room ceiling, now two stories high, a ragged funnel of splintered floorboards, bent copper pipes, and electrical wires that looked like severed veins bordering the walls and pointing towards him in the center of all of that sudden ruin. Voices murmured out in the kitchen.

George turned his head, hoping someone might be sitting just out of view, with a paper plate of potato salad and rolled slices of roast beef on her lap and a plastic cup of ginger ale in her hand. But the ruin persisted. He thought he called out, but the women's voices in the kitchen and the men's voices in the yard hummed uninterrupted. He lay on his heap of wreckage, looking up.

The second floor fell on him, with its unfinished pine framing and dead-end plumbing (the capped pipes never joined to the sink and toilet he had once intended to install) and racks of old coats and boxes of forgotten board games and puzzles and broken toys and bags of family pictures—some so old they were exposed on tin plates—all of it came crashing down into the cellar, he unable to even raise a hand to protect his face.

But he was nearly a ghost, almost made of nothing, and so the wood and metal and sheaves of brightly printed cardboard and paper (MOVE FORWARD SIX SPACES TO EASY STREET! Great-Grammy Noddin, shawled and stiff and frowning at the camera, absurd with her hat that looked like a sailor's funeral mound, heaped with flowers and netting), which otherwise would have crushed his bones, dropped on him and fell away like movie props, he or they facsimiles of former, actual things.

There he lay among the graduation photos and old wool jackets and rusted tools and newspaper clippings about his promotion to head of the mechanical-drawing department at the local high school, and then about his appointment as director of guidance, and then about his retirement and subsequent life as a trader and repairer of antique clocks. The mangled brass works of the clocks he had been repairing were strewn among the mess. He looked up three stories to the exposed support beams of the roof and the plump silver-backed batts of insulation that ran between them. One grandson or another (*which?*) had stapled the insulation into place years ago and now two or three lengths of it had come loose and lolled down like pink woolly tongues.

The roof collapsed, sending down a fresh avalanche of wood and nails, tarpaper and shingles and insulation. There was the sky, filled with flat-topped clouds, cruising like a fleet of anvils across the blue. George had the watery, raw feeling of being outdoors when you are sick. The clouds halted, paused for an instant, and plummeted onto his head.

The very blue of the sky followed, draining from the heights into that cluttered concrete socket. Next fell the stars, tinkling about him like the ornaments of heaven shaken loose. Finally, the black vastation itself came untacked and draped over the entire heap, covering George's confused obliteration.

Nearly seventy years before George died, his father, Howard Aaron Crosby, drove a wagon for his living. It was a wooden wagon. It was a chest of drawers mounted on two axles and wooden spoked wheels. There were dozens of drawers, each fitted with a recessed brass ring, pulled open with a hooked forefinger, that contained brushes and wood oil, tooth powder and nylon stockings, shaving soap and straight-edge razors. There were drawers with shoe shine and boot strings, broom handles and mop heads. There was a secret drawer where he kept four bottles of gin. Mostly, back roads were his route, dirt tracks that ran into the deep woods to hidden clearings where a log cabin sat among sawdust and tree stumps and a woman in a plain dress and hair pulled back so tight that she looked as if she were smiling (which she was not) stood in a crooked doorway with a cocked squirrel gun. Oh, it's you, Howard. Well, I guess I need one of your tin buckets. In the summer, he sniffed heather and sang *someone's rocking my dreamboat* and watched the monarch butterflies (butter fires, flutter flames; he imagined himself somewhat of a poet) up from Mexico. Spring and fall were his most prosperous times, fall because the backwoods people stocked up for the winter (he piled goods from the cart onto blazing maple leaves), spring because they had been out of supplies often for weeks before the roads were passable for his first rounds. Then they came to the wagon like sleepwalkers: bright-eyed and ravenous. Sometimes he came out of the woods with orders for coffins—a child, a wife wrapped up in burlap and stiff in the woodshed.

He tinkered. Tin pots, wrought iron. Solder melted and cupped in a clay dam. Quicksilver patchwork. Occasionally, a pot hammered back flat, the tinkle of tin sibilant, tiny beneath the lid of the boreal forest. Tinkerbird, coppersmith, but mostly a brush and mop drummer.

George could dig and pour the concrete basement for a house. He could saw the lumber and nail the frame. He could wire the rooms and fit the plumbing. He could hang the drywall. He could lay the floors and shingle the roof. He could build the brick steps. He could point the windows and paint the sashes. But he could not throw a ball or walk a mile; he hated exercise, and once he took early retirement at sixty he never had his heart rate up again if he could help it, and even then only if it were to whack through some heavy brush to get to a good trout pool. Lack of exercise might have been the reason that, when he had his first radiation treatment for the cancer in his groin, his legs swelled up like two dead seals on a beach and then turned as hard as lumber. Before he was bedridden, he walked as if he were an amputee from a war that predated modern prosthetics;

he tottered as if two hardwood legs hinged with iron pins were buckled to his waist. When his wife touched his legs at night in bed, through his pajamas, she thought of oak or maple and had to make herself think of something else in order not to imagine going down to his workshop in the basement and getting sandpaper and stain and sanding his legs and staining them with a brush, as if they belonged to a piece of furniture. Once, she snorted out loud, trying to stifle a laugh, when she thought, My husband, the table. She felt so bad afterward that she wept.

The stubbornness of some of the country women with whom Howard came into contact on his daily rounds cultivated in him, he believed, or would have believed, had he ever consciously thought about the matter, an unshakable, reasoning patience. When the soap company discontinued its old detergent for a new formula and changed the design on the box the soap came in, Howard had to endure debates he would have quickly conceded, were his adversaries not paying customers.

Where's the soap?

This is the soap.

The box is different.

Yes, they changed it.

What was wrong with the old box?

Nothing.

Why'd they change it?

Because the soap is better.

The soap is different?

Better.

Nothing wrong with the old soap.

Of course not, but this is better.

Nothing wrong with the old soap. How can it be better?

Well, it cleans better.

Cleaned fine before.

This cleans better—and faster.

Well, I'll just take a box of the normal soap.

This is the normal soap now.

I can't get my normal soap?

This is the normal soap; I guarantee it.

Well, I don't like to try a new soap.

It's not new.

Just as you say, Mr. Crosby. Just as you say.

Well, ma'am, I need another penny.

Another penny? For what?

The soap is a penny more, now that it's better.

I have to pay a penny more for different soap in a blue box? I'll just take a box of my normal soap.

George bought a broken clock at a tag sale. The owner gave him a reprint of an eighteenth-century repair manual for free. He began to poke around the guts of old clocks. As a machinist, he knew gear ratios, pistons and pinions, physics, the strength of materials. As a Yankee in North Shore horse country, he knew where the old money lay, dozing, dreaming of wool mills and slate quarries, ticker tape and foxhunts. He found that bankers paid well to keep their balky heirlooms telling time. He could replace the worn tooth on a strike wheel by hand. Lay the clock facedown. Unscrew the screws; maybe just pull them from the cedar or walnut case, the threads long since turned to wood dust dusted from mantels. Lift off the back of the clock like the lid of a treasure chest. Bring the long-armed jeweler's lamp closer, to just over your shoulder. Examine the dark brass. See the pinions gummed up with dirt and oil. Look at the blue and green and purple ripples of metal hammered, bent, torched. Poke your finger into the clock; fiddle the escape wheel (every part perfectly named—escape: the end of the machine, the place where the energy leaks out, breaks free, beats time). Stick your nose closer; the metal smells tannic. Read the names etched onto the works: *Ezra Bloxham–1794; Geo. E. Tiggs–1832; Thos. Flatchbart–1912.* Lift the darkened works from the case. Lower them into ammonia. Lift them out, nose burning, eyes watering, and see them shine and star through your tears. File the teeth. Punch the bushings. Load the springs. Fix the clock. Add your name.

Tinker, tinker. Tin, tin, tin. Tintinnabulation. There was the ring of pots and buckets. There was also the ring in Howard Crosby's ears, a ring that began at a dis-

tance and came closer, until it sat in his ears, then bur-
rowed into them. His head thrummed as if it were a
clapper in a bell. Cold hopped onto the tips of his toes
and rode on the ripples of the ringing throughout his
body until his teeth clattered and his knees faltered and
he had to hug himself to keep from unraveling. This
was his *aura*, a cold halo of chemical electricity that
encircled him immediately before he was struck by a full
seizure. Howard had epilepsy. His wife, Kathleen, formerly Kathleen Black, of the Quebec Blacks but from a
reduced and stern branch of the family, cleared aside
chairs and tables and led him to the middle of the
kitchen floor. She wrapped a stick of pine in a napkin for
him to bite so he would not swallow or chew off his
tongue. If the fit came fast, she crammed the bare stick
between his teeth and he would wake to a mouthful of
splintered wood and the taste of sap, his head feeling
like a glass jar full of old keys and rusty screws.

To reassemble the dismantled clock, the back plate of
the works is laid upon a bed of soft cloth, preferably
thick chamois folded many times. Each wheel and its
arbor is inserted into its proper hole, beginning with
the great wheel and its loose-fitting fusee, that
grooved cone of wonder given to mankind by Mr. Da
Vinci, and proceeding to the smallest, the teeth of one
meshing with the gear collar of the next, and so on
until the flywheel of the strike train and the escape

wheel of the going train are fitted into their rightful places. Now, the horologist looks upon an open-faced, fairy-book contraption; gears lean to and fro like a lazy machine in a dream. The universe's time cannot be marked thusly. Such a crooked and flimsy device could only keep the fantastic hours of unruly ghosts. The front plate of the works is taken in hand and fitted first onto the upfacing arbors of the main and strike springs, these being the largest and most easily fitted of the sundry parts. This accomplished, the horologist then lifts the rickety sandwich of loose guts to eye level, holding the works approximately together by squeezing the two plates, taking care to apply neither too much pressure (thus damaging the finer of the unaligned arbor ends) nor too little (thus causing the half-re-formed machine to disassemble itself back into its various constituent parts, which often flee to dusty and obscure nooks throughout the horologist's workshop, causing much profaning and blasphemy). If, when the patient horologist has finished his attempt and the clock, when thumbed at the great wheel, does squeak and gibber rather than hum and whir with brass logic, this process must be reversed and tried again with calm reason until the imps of disorder are banished. Of clocks with only a going train, reanimating the machine is simple. More sophisticated contraptions, such as those fashioned with extra abilities, like a pantomime of the moon or a model fool juggling fruit, require an almost infinite skill and doggedness. (The author has heard of a clock supposedly seen in eastern Bohemia that had the likeness of a great oak tree wrought in iron and brass around its dial. As the seasons of its homeland changed, the branches of the tree turned a thousand tiny copper leaves, each threaded on a hair-thin spindle, from enameled green to metallic red. Then, by astounding mechanisms within the case (fashioned to look like one of the mythical pillars once believed to hold up the earth) the branches released the leaves to spiral down their threads and strew themselves about the lower part of the clock-face. If this machine in fact existed, Mr. Newton himself could not have sat beneath a more amazing tree.)

—from *The Reasonable Horologist*,
by the Rev. Kenner Davenport, 1783

George Crosby remembered many things as he died, but in an order he could not control. To look at his life, to take the stock he always imagined a man would at his end, was to witness a shifting mass, the tiles of a mosaic spinning, swirling, reportraying, always in recognizable swaths of colors, familiar elements, molecular units, intimate currents, but also independent now of his will, showing him a different self every time he tried to make an assessment.

* * *

One hundred and sixty-eight hours before he died, he snaked into the basement window of the West Cove Methodist Church and rang the bell on Halloween night. He waited in the basement for his father to whip him for doing it. His father laughed so hard and slapped his own thigh, because George had stuffed the seat of his pants with old *Saturday Evening Posts*. He sat at dinner silent, afraid to look at his mother because it was eleven o'clock at night and his father wasn't home and still his mother made them sit in front of cold food. He married. He moved. He was a Methodist, a Congregationalist, and finally a Unitarian. He drew machines and taught mechanical drawing and had heart attacks and survived, sped down the new highway before it opened with his friends from engineering school, taught math, got a master's degree in education, counseled guidance in high school, went back north every summer to fly-fish with his poker buddies—doctors, cops, music teachers—bought a broken clock at a tag sale and a reprint of an eighteenth-century manual on how to fix it, retired, went on group tours to Asia, to Europe, to Africa, fixed clocks for thirty years, spoiled his grandkids, got Parkinson's, got diabetes, got cancer, and was laid out in a hospital bed in the middle of his living room, right where they put the dining room table, fitted with its two extra leaves for holiday dinners.

George never permitted himself to imagine his father. Occasionally, though, when he was fixing a clock,

when a new spring he was coaxing into its barrel came
loose from its arbor and exploded, cutting his hands,
sometimes damaging the rest of the works, he had a
vision of his father on the floor, his feet kicking chairs,
bunching up rugs, lamps falling off of their tables, his
head banging on floorboards, his teeth clamped onto a
stick or George's own fingers.

His mother had lived with him and his family until
she died. Upon occasion, at meals mostly, maybe because
that was the site of her being preempted, outsmarted by
her former husband, left at the dinner table with her
plans to have him taken away, she would recall what a
frivolous man his father had been. At breakfast, she
scooped oatmeal into her mouth and pulled the spoon
from the clutches of her dentures with a stupendous
clanking and sucking and would say something like, A
poet, ha! He was a birdbrain, a magpie, a loony bird,
flapping around with those fits and all.

But George forgave his mother her contrary heart.
Whenever he thought about what her bitter laments
sought to stanch, he was overtaken by tears and paused,
looking up from the headlines of the morning paper, to
lean over and kiss her camphored brow. To which gesture she would say, Don't you try to make me feel better! That man cast a shadow forever over my peace of
mind. The damned fool! And even that would make
George feel good; her incessant litanies soothed her and
reminded her that that life was over.

As he lay on his deathbed, George wanted to see his father again. He wanted to imagine his father. Each time he tried to concentrate and go back, tried to burrow deep and far away from the present, a pain, a noise, someone rolling him from side to side to change his sheets, the toxins leaking from his cancer-clogged kidneys into his thickening and darkening blood, reeled him back to his worn-out body and scrambled mind.

One afternoon, in the spring before his death, George, his illnesses consolidating, decided to dictate memories and anecdotes from his life into a tape recorder. His wife was out shopping and so he took the recorder down to his work desk in the basement. He opened the door between his workshop and tool shop. There was a woodstove in the tool shop, between the drill press and metal lathe. He crumpled up some old newspaper and put it in the stove, along with three logs from the half cord of wood he kept stacked in a remote corner of the shop, near the door to the bulkhead. He lit a fire and adjusted the flue, hoping to warm the concretey chill of the basement. He returned to his desk in the workshop. There was a cheap microphone plugged into the tape machine that would not stay upright on the clip collared around it. The clip was so light that the twist in the wire running from the microphone to the recorder kept flicking it over. George tried to straighten the wire, but the microphone would not stand, so he merely placed it on top of the tape recorder. The levers on the recorder were heavy and required some effort to push down before they clicked into place. Each was labeled with a cryptic abbreviation and George had to experiment with them before he felt confident he had found the right combination for recording his voice. The tape in the recorder had a faded pink label upon which had been typed, Early Blues Compilation, Copyright Hal Broughton, Jaw Creek, Pennsylvania. George recalled that he and his wife had bought the tape at one or another of the Elderhostel college courses they had taken during one or another summer years ago. When George first pressed the PLAY lever, a man's voice, thin and remote, warbled about a hellhound on his trail. Rather than rewind the tape, George felt that such a complaint might be a good introduction to his talk, so he just began recording. He leaned forward into the microphone with his arms crossed and resting on the edge of the desk, as if he were answering questions at a hearing. He began formally: My name is George Washington Crosby. I was born in West Cove, Maine, in the year 1915. I moved to Enon, Massachusetts, in 1936. And so on. After these statistics, he found that he could think only of doggerel and slightly obscene anecdotes to tell, mostly having to do with foolish stunts undertaken after drinking too much whiskey during a fishing trip and often enough centered around running into a warden with a creel full of trout and no fishing license, or a pistol that a doctor had brought into the woods: If that pistol is nine millimeters, I'll kiss your bare, frozen ass right out here on the ice; the lyrics to a song called Come Around, Mother, It's Better When You're Awake. And so forth. But after a handful of such stories, he began to talk about his father and his mother, his brother, Joe, and his sisters, about taking night courses to finish school and about becoming a father. He talked about blue snow and barrels of apples and splitting frozen wood so brittle that it rang when you split it. He talked about what it is like to be a grandparent for the first time and to think about what it is you will leave behind when you die. By the time the tape ran out an hour and a half later (after he had flipped it over once, almost without being conscious of doing so), and the RECORD button sprang up with a buzz, he was openly weeping and lamenting the loss of this world of light and hope. So deeply moved, he pulled the cassette from the machine, flipped it back over to the beginning, fitted it back into its snug carriage of capstans and guiding pins, and pressed PLAY, thinking that he might preserve such a mood of pure, clean sorrow by listening back to his narrative. He imagined that his memoirs might now sound like those of an admirable stranger, a person he did not know but whom he immediately recognized and loved dearly. Instead, the voice he heard sounded nasally and pinched and, worse, not very well educated, as if he were a bumpkin who had been called, perhaps even

in mockery, to testify about holy things, as if not the tes-
timony but the fumbling through it were the reason for
his presence in front of some dire, heavenly senate. He
listened to six seconds of the tape before he ejected it
and threw it into the fire burning in the woodstove.

Saw grass and wildflowers grew high along the spines of
the dirt roads and brushed the belly of Howard's wagon.
Bears pawed fruit in the bushes along the ruts.

   Howard had a pine display case, fastened by fake
leather straps and stained to look like walnut. Inside, on
fake velvet, were cheap gold-plated earrings and pen-
dants of semiprecious stones. He opened this case for
haggard country wives when their husbands were off
chopping trees or reaping the back acres. He showed
them the same half-dozen pieces every year the last time
he came around, when he thought, This is the season—
preserving done, woodpile high, north wind up and getting cold, night showing up earlier every day, dark and
ice pressing down from the north, down on the raw
wood of their cabins, on the rough-cut rafters that sag
and sometimes snap from the weight of the dark and the
ice, burying families in their sleep, the dark and the ice
and sometimes the red in the sky through trees: the
heartbreak of a cold sun. He thought, Buy the pendant,
sneak it into your hand from the folds of your dress and
let the low light of the fire lap at it late at night as you
wait for the roof to give out or your will to snap and the

ice to be too thick to chop through with the ax as you
stand in your husband's boots on the frozen lake at midnight, the dry hack of the blade on ice so tiny under the
wheeling and frozen stars, the soundproof lid of heaven,
that your husband would never stir from his sleep in the
cabin across the ice, would never hear and come running, half-frozen, in only his union suit, to save you from
chopping a hole in the ice and sliding into it as if it were
a blue vein, sliding down into the black, silty bottom of
the lake, where you would see nothing, would perhaps
feel only the stir of some somnolent fish in the murk as
the plunge of you in your wool dress and the big boots
disturbed it from its sluggish winter dreams of ancient
seas. Maybe you would not even feel that, as you struggled in clothes that felt like cooling tar, and as you
slowed, calmed, even, and opened your eyes and looked
for a pulse of silver, an imbrication of scales, and as you
closed your eyes again and felt their lids turn to slippery,
ichthyic skin, the blood behind them suddenly cold, and
as you found yourself not caring, wanting, finally, to
rest, finally wanting nothing more than the sudden,
new, simple hum threading between your eyes. The ice
is far too thick to chop through. You will never do it.
You could never do it. So buy the gold, warm it with
your skin, slip it onto your lap when you are sitting by
the fire and all you will otherwise have to look at is your
splintery husband gumming chew or the craquelure of
your own chapped hands.

No woman ever bought a piece of jewelry. One might lift a pendant from its bed and rub it between her fingers. She would say, It sure is, when he said, Well, now, that's a beautiful piece. Sometimes he saw a woman's face seize for the slightest part of a second, the jewelry stirring some half-forgotten personal hope, some dream from the distant cusp of marriage. Or her breath would hitch, as if something long hung on a nail or staked to a chain seemed to uncatch, but only for a second. The woman would hand back the trinket he offered. No, no, I guess not, Howard. Case slipped back into its drawer, he would turn his cart around in the yard and start back out of the woods, winter already sealing the country people in behind him.

The local agent for Howard's supplies was a man named Cullen. Cullen was a hustler. One day a month, he sat at a table in the back room at Sander's store and rooked his agent of his due. He spread Howard's receipts for the month out across the table and leaned forward and looked at them through the smoke of the cigarette that always dangled from his lip. When he did this, Howard always thought that the agent looked like he was dealing cards for a hand of poker or a magic trick. Cullen squinted at the receipts: Only five boxes of lye; need six to make discount. Ten cotton mop heads. Good, but my cost went up. Need to sell a dozen now. You get a nickel less than before. What about that new soap? I don't care it's tough to convert these backwoods biddies; you're a salesman. What the hell are you doing out there? Sniffing daisies? Godammit, Crosby, what are you doing with those iceboxes and washing machines? How many brochures have you handed out? I don't give a good goddamn if they don't understand installment plans—installment is the *future*; it is the *grail* of selling! Cullen scooped up the receipts and crammed them into his case. He reached into his pocket and pulled out a roll of money. He peeled a ten and seven ones out of the roll. He dug in his other pocket and pitched a fistful of change onto the table (like dice, Howard thought) and flicked fifty-seven cents' worth of coins out of the pile with a forefinger and put the rest back in his pocket so quickly, it was as if that, too, were one of his tricks. Sign here. Crosby, how are you going to be one of my twelve? This was the part of every meeting with the agent that Howard dreaded—when Cullen quoted Bruce Barton. Who was the greatest businessman ever, Crosby? The greatest salesman? Advertiser? Who? Howard looked at the knot in Cullen's cheap tie and smiled, trying not to look put out but trying not to answer the question, either. Come on, Crosby. Haven't you read the book? I practically gave it to you for cost! Howard sighed and said, It was Jesus. That's right, the agent said, half getting out of his chair, pounding a fist on the table, pointing a finger out toward heaven, past the new snowshoes hanging high on the walls. Jesus!

Jesus was the founder of modern business, he quoted. *He was the most popular dinner guest in Jerusalem. He picked up twelve men from the bottom ranks of business and forged them into an organization that conquered the world!* How are you going to be one of my twelve, Crosby, if you can't sell, if you are not *on fire to sell?*

One hundred and thirty-two hours before he died, George awoke from the racket of the collapsing universe to the darkness of night and a silence, which, once the clamor of his nightmares faded, he could not understand. The room was lit only by a small pewter lamp set on one of the end tables near the couch. The couch ran along the length of the hospital bed. At the far end of the couch, leaning toward the light on the table, sat one of his grandsons, reading a book.

George said, Charlie.

Charlie said, Gramp, and put the paperback book on his lap.

George said, Why so damn quiet?

Charlie said, It's late.

George said, Is that right? Still seems awful damn quiet. George turned his head to the left and then right. To the left was the Queen Anne armchair and the fire-place in which he had not built a fire for thirty years, not since he quit smoking pipes. He remembered the pipe tree he had kept in the basement, at his work desk. At first he had imagined his enthusiasm for pipes to be

like that which he had for clocks; he had bought the
pipe tree at a flea market in Newburyport. How do I
remember this? he thought in the bed, concerned with
parsing the quality of the silence he experienced almost
as a noise, of finding its source, and, instead, here was
the flea market in Newburyport and the table of junk
with the pipe tree and what the old crook who ran the
table looked like (some sort of retired sailor or mer-
chant seaman, with an Irish sweater and Greek fishing
cap) and sounded like (salt-cured Yankee via Bangor via
Cape Breton) and almost every item on the table
(rusted trowels, eyeless dolls, empty tobacco tins, flaking sheaves of sheet music, a candy thermometer, a statue
of Christopher Columbus) and how he had bartered
with the man for the tree (How close to ten cents would
you take for that pipe tree? Five bucks! How'd a thief
like you get in here? Two bucks? Well, you'd better hold
on to it a while longer. A dollar and a quarter? Sold.).
He bought a dozen pipes from various collectors. He
put them in the tree, with the intention of cultivating a
taste for a range of expensive tobaccos and using each
pipe for one type of tobacco only. Within a week, he
smoked the cheapest house blend from the local tobac-
conist in a pipe he had bartered as part of a deal for a
box full of clock parts, and which, when an occasional
puff tasted sour, he suspected of being made not from
wood, but plastic. He smoked bowl after bowl of cheap
shag while he fixed clocks. At the end of the day, after

dinner, he sat in the Queen Anne chair (which he had bought cheaply at an estate sale because two of its legs were broken) by the fire and smoked the last bowl of the day. When he developed a precancerous blister on his lower lip, he threw out his pipes and the tree and the tins of tobacco and contented himself with smoking half of an occasional cigar when he had to sweep dead leaves out of the garage. Although he had not sat in the Queen Anne chair since he quit smoking his pipes, there remained a sort of shadow of his outline on the fabric of the chair's backrest; it was not so much a stain as a silhouette of just slightly darker fabric, which could be seen in just the right light from just the right angle, and which still would have fit his shape perfectly, had he been able to rise from his sickbed and sit in the chair.

His head was propped up with pillows. In front of him, at the foot of the bed, he could see a narrow part of the Persian rug that covered the floor. Beyond the rug, at the far wall, was the dining table, with its leaves taken out and its wings lowered. It ran nearly the width of the wall. At either end of the table was a ladder-back chair with a cane seat. Hanging above the table (on which there was always a bowl of wooden fruit or a crystal vase of silk flowers) was a still life done in oil. It was a dim, murky scene, lit perhaps by a single candle not visible within the frame, of a table on which lay a silver fish and a dark loaf of bread on a cutting board, a round of ruddy cheese, a bisected orange with both halves arranged with their cross sections facing the viewer, a drinking goblet made of green glass, with a wide spiral stem and what looked like glass buttons fixed around the base of the broad cup. A large part of the cup had been broken and dimly glinting slivers of glass lay around the base. There was a pewter-handled knife on the cutting board, in front of the fish and the loaf. There was also a black rod of some sort, with a white tip, running parallel to the knife. No one had ever been able to figure out what the rod actually was. A grand-child once remarked that it looked like a magician's wand, and, in fact, the object did resemble the type of wand that amateurs use to conjure rabbits or make pitchers of water disappear into their top hats at chil-dren's birthday parties. But the rest of the picture, no matter how recently or distantly it had been painted, was by influence or origin Dutch or Flemish, and the rod certainly not a pun or clever joke. And so it remained a small household mystery, which the family was content to puzzle over now and then for a moment when they were waiting for someone to get his coat on, or were daydreaming on the couch during a winter afternoon, and which no one cared to research.

To his right, past the right end of the dining table and the chair next to it, was the small entryway, which con-sisted of the doorway into the living room, the front door on the right, the door to the coat closet on the far side, and the door to the unfinished attic (which, when he had built the house fifty years before, George had fitted for plumbing and electricity, with the intention of eventually making the space into a single large family room) on the left. To the right of that was a rolltop desk, in which George kept bills and receipts and unused ledger books. There was another oil painting hanging above the desk, this one of a packet schooner sailing out of Gloucester in stormy weather. It was a scene of roiling dark greens and blues and grays swarming around the lines of the ship, which was seen from the rear. The insides of the very tips of the waves were illuminated from within by a sourceless light. If you watched the straight lines of the schooner's masts and rigging (storm up, the ship was not under sail) long enough in the dim light of an early evening or on a rainy day, the sea would begin to move at the corners of your vision. They would stop the moment you looked directly at them, only to slither and snake again when you returned your gaze to the ship.

Directly to George's right was the blue couch and its end tables, where his grandson sat, now looking at him, book in lap. Behind the couch, there was a large bay window, which looked out onto the front lawn and the street behind the couch, but heavy curtains, which his wife had kept closed day and night since he had come home to die, obscured it. The curtains were as thick and heavy as those of a theater. They were cream-colored, with broad vertical pillars of a maroon so dark it was almost black. The pillars were festooned with leafy tendrils that spiraled up and down their lengths. In between the diagonals of the bunting were alternating images of songbirds with scraps of ribbon or grass in their beaks and of marble urns. Looking at the curtains, it seemed to George that his grandson sat in front of a small, obscured stage and that he might at any moment stand up, step aside, and, with arm outstretched in introduction, present some sort of puppet show.

Instead, the grandson said again, You okay, Gramp? Awful damn quiet.

When he could not turn his head any farther, he had to imagine the rest of the room behind him. There was the console television, the red velvet love seat, the hand-colored photograph of his wife taken when she was seventeen, set in an oval rosewood frame, and there was the grandfather's clock.

That was it, he realized; the clock had run down. All of the clocks in the room had wound down—the tambours and carriage clocks on the mantel, the banjo and mirror and Viennese regulator on the walls, the Chelsea ship's bells on the rolltop desk, the ogee on the end table, and the seven-foot walnut-cased Stevenson grandfather's clock, made in Nottingham in 1801, with its moon-phase window on the dial and pair of robins threading flowery buntings around the Roman numerals. When he imagined inside the case of that clock, dark and dry and hollow, and the still pendulum hanging down its length, he felt the inside of his own chest and had a sudden panic that it, too, had wound down.

When his grandchildren had been little, they had asked if they could hide inside the clock. Now he wanted to gather them and open himself up and hide them among his ribs and faintly ticking heart.

When he realized that the silence by which he had been confused was that of all of his clocks having been allowed to wind down, he understood that he was going to die in the bed where he lay.

Clocks are all stopped, he croaked to his grandson.

Nana said it would drive you mad.

(In truth, his wife had said that the ticking, never mind the chimes, drove *her* mad and that she could not bear the vigil with all of that clatter. In actual truth, his wife was soothed by the sound of ticking clocks and their chimes, and for many years after her husband's death, in the condominium she bought at a retirement complex with the cash he had hidden away for her in the basement and in half a dozen safety-deposit boxes located around the North Shore, she kept a dozen of the finest pieces from his collection running and arranged around her living room in such a way that they seemed, in their precise alignment, with which she fussed and fine-tuned for months, to strike a chord that nearly conjured her dead husband, almost invoked him in the room; he always seemed just out of sight among the ticks and tocks and, at midnight, when she lay alone in her canopy bed and all of the clocks struck twelve at the same time, she knew without a doubt that her fastidious ghost of a husband was drifting around in the living room, inspecting each machine through his bifocals, making sure that they were all even of beat, adjusted and precise.)

Drive me mad nothing, he said. Get up and wind them. And so the young person, whose name he could not recall, moved from clock to clock and wound each one.

But not the striking trains, the young person said. It'd be too loud; we'd raise hell if all of these things struck; Nana would kill us.

George said, Okay, okay, and the blood in his veins and the breath in his chest seemed to go easier as he heard the ratchet and click of the springs being wound and the rising chorus of clocks, which did not seem to him to tick but to breathe and to give one another comfort by merely being in one another's presence, like a gathering of people at a church dinner or at a slide show held in the local library.

Besides fixing pots and selling soap, these are some of the things that Howard did at one time or another on his rounds, sometimes to earn extra money, mostly not: shoot a rabid dog, deliver a baby, put out a fire, pull a rotten tooth, cut a man's hair, sell five gallons of homemade whiskey for a backwoods bootlegger named Potts, fish a drowned child from a creek.

The drowned child was the daughter of a widow named La Rose. She had been playing at the edge of the creek and slipped on a wet stone and split her head and passed out facedown in the water. The current had tugged her farther into the water, carried her for several hundred feet, and then deposited her on a sandbar in the middle of the creek. Howard took his shoes off and rolled up his trouser legs and waded out to the child. When he first bent to lift her, he did so as if to hoist an errant lamb onto his hip, but when he put his arms under the little body and felt its cold and saw its hair trailing in the current and thought of the child's mother standing behind him on the bank, he turned her face up and raised her and carried her as if she were asleep and he taking her from the back of a wagon to her pallet bed near the woodstove after returning from a trip visiting relatives.

The man whose hair he cut was named Melish. He was nineteen years old and due to be married in an hour and a half. His mother was dead; his sisters and brothers, all much older than he, were married off already and gone to Canada or New Hampshire or south to Woonsocket. His father was plowing their fifteen acres of potatoes and would have just as soon scalped the boy as cut his hair, because him getting married meant the last helping hands were abandoning the farm. Howard took a pair of shears and a medium-size tin pot from his wagon. He fitted the pot over the boy's head and cut in a circle around its circumference. When he was done, he took a hand mirror from its wrapping paper and gave

it to the boy. The boy turned his head left and then
right and handed the mirror back to Howard. He said,
I guess that looks pretty smart, Mr. Crosby.

The man whose tooth he pulled was named Gilbert.
Gilbert was a hermit who lived deep in the woods along
the Penobscot River. He seemed not to live in any shelter other than the woods themselves, although some
men who hunted in the woods for deer and bear and
moose speculated that he might live in some forgotten
trapper's cabin. Others thought he might live in a tree
house of some sort, or at least a lean-to. In all the years
he was known to live in the forest, never had a winter
hunting party seen so much as the ashes from a fire or a
single footprint. No one could imagine how a man
could survive one winter alone and exposed in the
woods, never mind decades of them. Howard, instead of
trying to explain the hermit's existence in terms of
hearth fires and trappers' shacks, preferred the blank
space the old man actually seemed to inhabit; he liked
to think of some fold in the woods, some seam that only
the hermit could sense and slip into, where the ice and
snow, where the frozen forest itself, would accept him
and he would no longer need fire or wool blankets, but
instead flourish wreathed in snow, spun in frost, with limbs
like cold wood and blood like frigid sap.

Gilbert was a graduate of Bowdoin College. According to the stories, he had liked to boast that he had been a
classmate of Nathaniel Hawthorne's. Although he would

have to be nearly 120 years old for the rumor to be true, no one cared to refute the claim, because they found too delightful to dispel the notion that the local hermit, dressed in animal skins, muttering litanies (as often as not in Latin), and, in warmer seasons, attended by a small but avid swarm of flies, which constantly buzzed around his head, crawled over his nose, and sipped the tears from the corners of his eyes, had once been a clean-faced, well-ironed acquaintance of the author of *The Scarlet Letter*. Gilbert was apparently not his real name and no one really knew when he had been born so the people left it at that.

People liked to speculate and tell stories about Gilbert the Hermit, especially when they sat around their wood-stoves on winter nights with a blizzard howling outside; the thought of him out there in the maelstrom gave them a comforting thrill.

Howard supplied Gilbert. Gilbert's needs from the world of men were few, but he did require needles and thread, twine, and tobacco. Once a year, on the first day that the ice went out of the ponds, sometime in May, Howard rode his wagon to the Camp Comfort Club hunting cabin, itself remote, and from there toted on his back the supplies he knew Gilbert required down an old Indian trail that followed the river. Somewhere along the way, Howard would meet Gilbert. The men would greet one another with nods of their heads. They struggled through the bushes down to the river's edge, Howard

with his bundle, Gilbert with his court of flies and a
buckskin bag. There they would each find a rock or a dry
tuft of grass to sit on. Howard took a tin of tobacco from
the bundle of supplies he had brought for Gilbert and
handed it to the hermit. Gilbert held the open tin to his
nose and inhaled slowly, savoring the rich, sweet near
dampness of the new tobacco; by the time he met
Howard each year, he was down to the last flakes of his
supply. Howard imagined that the fragrance of new
tobacco was a sort of confirmation to Gilbert that he had
indeed lived another year, endured another winter in the
woods. After smelling the tobacco and looking out at the
river for a moment, Gilbert held out his hand to Howard.
Howard took a pipe from one of his jacket pockets and
gave it to the hermit. Howard did not otherwise smoke
and kept the pipe for this one bowlful a year. Gilbert
packed Howard's pipe and then his own (which was
beautiful—carved from a burl of dark red wood and
which Howard imagined belonging once, long ago, in a
brass stand on a dean's desk) and the two men smoked
together in silence and watched the waters rush. While
he smoked, Gilbert's flock of flies temporarily dispersed,
but seemingly without rancor or resentment. When the
pipes were spent, each man tapped the ashes out against
his rock and put his pipe away. The flies settled back in
their orbit around the hermit's head (*Circum capit*, he
muttered) and he opened his buckskin bag and produced
two crude wooden carvings, one which seemed to be a

moose, the other a beaver, or perhaps a woodchuck, or even a groundhog. The work was so poor that Howard could only say for sure that the little raw wooden lumps that the hermit placed in the winter-dead grass between them were supposed to be animals of some kind. Next to the carvings, Gilbert then lay a beautifully skinned fox fur, head included, that smelled like rotting meat. There was a moment of panic for the flies as they decided which was more rancid, the hermit or the skin. In the end, they were loyal to their more pungent, living host. Howard placed the bundle of supplies on the grass and each man collected his goods. The men had exchanged few words during the first few years of this spring ritual and these only to refine the order of Gilbert's supplies. One year he said, More needles. Another year he said, No more tea—coffee now. Once the list had been refined and finally established, the men no longer spoke at all. For the past seven years, neither man had uttered a single word to the other.

The last year Howard met Gilbert in the woods, though, the men spoke. When he came upon the hermit, he saw that the man's left cheek was as swollen and as shiny as a ripe apple. Gilbert shuffled his feet and stared at the ground and held his hand against the cheek. Even the flies were solicitous of their sponsor's pain and seemed to buzz more gingerly about him. Howard cocked his head in a silent question.

Gilbert whispered, Tooth.

Howard could not imagine that this old husk of a man, this recluse who seemed not much more than a sour hank of hair and rags, had a tooth left in his head to ache. Nevertheless, it was true. Stepping closer, Gilbert opened his mouth and Howard, squinting to get a good look, saw in that dank, ruined purple cavern, stuck way in the back of an otherwise-empty levy of gums, a single black tooth planted in a swollen and bright red throne of flesh. A breeze caught the hermit's breath and Howard gasped and saw visions of slaughter-houses and dead pets under porches.

Tooth, the hermit said again, and pointed into his mouth.

Oh, yes, awful thing, Howard said, and smiled in sympathy.

The hermit said, No! Tooth! and continued pointing. Howard realized that the poor afflicted man wanted him to take the tooth out.

Oh, no, no! he said. I have no idea—

Gilbert cut him off. No! Tooth! he squeaked, an octave higher than before.

But I haven't any— Again the hermit cut him off, shooing him back toward where his wagon stood, three miles away at the Comfort Camp Club cabin.

Howard returned two and a half hours later with a small flask of corn whiskey from Potts's mountainside still and a pair of long-handled pliers he used when he had to solder small pieces of tin to leaky pots. At first,

Gilbert refused any liquor, but when Howard grabbed the tooth with the plicrs, the old man passed out. Howard dashed a handful of cold river water on Gilbert's face. The hermit came to and motioned for the whiskey, which he drank in a single draft, then passed out again from the alcohol on the bedeviled tooth. Another splash of water revived Gilbert, and the two men sat for a time watching a pair of sparrows chase a crow above the fir trees on the other side of the river.

The river was high after an early, fast melt, and loud. Voices seemed to mingle in the water, as if there were a race of men who dwelled among the rapids. When Gilbert began to list and recite Virgil, *Uere nouo, gelidus canis cum montibus humor liquitur,* Howard reached into the hermit's mouth with the pliers, grabbed the fetid tooth, and pulled with all of his strength. The tooth did not budge. Howard let go. Gilbert looked baffled for a moment and then passed out again, flat on his back, the flies neatly following him from upright to laid out. Howard was convinced at first that his customer was dead, but a damp whistle from the hermit's fly-rimmed nose indicated that he could still be counted among the relatively quick.

The old man's mouth hung wide open. Howard straddled his shoulders and grabbed the tooth with the pliers. When he finally succeeded in excavating the tooth, Gilbert's face and beard were covered in blood. Another splash of river water revived the patient. When he saw Howard standing before him with the gory pliers in one hand and a tooth extraordinarily long of root in the other, Gilbert fainted.

Two weeks later, Buddy the Dog's barking wakened Howard. He rose from bed and went to the kitchen door to see if there was a bear or stray cow in the yard. Placed on the doorstep was a package wrapped in greasy, foul-smelling leather and tied with twine which Howard recognized as the type he sold. Standing in the moonlight, he untied the twine and unfolded the leather. Beneath the leather was a layer of red velvet. Howard opened the velvet and there, looking as new as the day it was printed, the pages uncut, was a copy of *The Scarlet Letter*. Howard opened the book. Inscribed on the title page were the words *To "Hick" Gilbert: Here is to the shared memories of young men in the prime of their journeys. Yours always in faith and brotherly friendship, Nath'l Hawthorne, 1852.*

When the ice went out the next year, Howard took his pipe from its drawer in the wagon and rubbed it across the thigh of his pants and blew into the bowl and put it in his jacket pocket. He made up a bundle of Gilbert's supplies and hiked along the Indian trail. There was no sign of the hermit. Howard made the hike every day for a week, but Gilbert never appeared. On the seventh day, Howard turned off the trail and sat by the river and smoked a pipeful of the tobacco that he had packed for the hermit. As he smoked, he listened to the voices in the rapids. They murmured about a place somewhere deep in the woods where a set of bones lay on a bed of moss, above which a troop of mournful flies had kept vigil the previous autumn until the frosts came and they, too, had succumbed.

This is a book. It is a book I found in a box. I found the box in the attic. The box was in the attic, under the eaves. The attic was hot and still. The air was stale with dust. The dust was from old pictures and books. The dust in the air was made up of the book I found. I breathed the book before I saw it; tasted the book before I read it. The book has a red marbled cover. It has large pages. The pages are made of heavy paper the color of blanched almonds. The book is filled with writing. The writing is in blue ink. The ink is heavy and built up in places the way paint builds up on canvas. The paper did not absorb the ink. The ink had to dry before the book was closed or a page turned. The blue of the ink is so dark that it looks black. It is only in flourishes tailing off of serifs or in lines where the hand lessened its pressure on the pen that you can see the blue. The handwriting looks like yours. It looks like you wrote the book. It is a dictionary or an encyclopedia of some sort. The book is full of reports from the backs of events, full of weak, cold light from the north, small constructions from short summers. Let me read you an example. Are you comfortable? Do you want the bed down a little bit more? Would you like some water? No; every one else is asleep. Shall I read you an example? You don't remember writing this? The handwriting looks very much like yours. Very much like mine, too, with the *f*'s that look like elongated *s*'s with dashes through their middles. And the mix of script and printing. Why don't I start at the beginning, with the first entry? No, I'm Charlie. Sam is at our mother's getting some sleep. No, I don't think he smokes anymore, no. Not since he got pneumonia last winter. Yes, we sure have; we've always had family no matter what. This first one is

> *Cosmos Borealis:* Light skin of sky and cloud and mountain on the still pond. Water body beneath teeming with reeds and silt and trout (sealed in day skin and night skin and ice lids), which we draw out with silk threads, fitted with snags of fur or bright feathers. Skin like glass like liquid like skin; our words scrieved the slick surface (reflecting risen moon, spinning stars, flitting bats), so that we had only to whisper across the wide plate. Green drakes blossomed powder dry among the stars, glowing white, out of pods, which rose from the muck at the bottom of the pond and broke open on the skin of the water. We whispered across the galaxies, Who needs Mars?

What is it like to be full of lightning? What is it like to be split open from the inside by lightning? Howard used to imagine that it was like the rupture of a fit. Although he never remembered them, he had the sense that, although there was cold before and chills after, during his seizures his blood boiled and his brain nearly fried in its skull pan. It was as if there were a secret door that opened on its own to an electric storm spinning somewhere out on the fringes of the solar system. He imagined the door. Closed, it was invisible, cloaked in the colors of the world (it was outside; it moved). Open, it was made of thick plain oak and swung outward. It had a wooden knob because the electricity on the other side would erupt from a metal handle. Howard often wondered if there was a knob on the outside of the door. In his mind, he could not see if there was because the door was either closed and hidden or flung open, so that the front, the side painted in light and shadow, grass and water, faced the opposite direction. The opened doorway framed an unbounded darkness. There was the black of the universe surrounding a pinwheel of light. Needles of electricity forked out of the whirlpool of sparks. Most of this lightning flashed and was gone in an instant. But when one of the charges found its way through the door and into Howard, it stuck fast; it latched onto something inside of him and held and held. In the cold, blasted, numb hours following a seizure, confusion prevailed; Howard's blistered brain crackled and sparked blue behind his eyes and he sat slumped, slack-jawed, blanket-wrapped, baffled by his diet of lightning. It was as if some well-intending being desired to give him a special gift and spoon-fed him the voltage from behind the door. No, not being, even. There was the door, or maybe the doors, or maybe not even doors, just the curtains and murals of this world and the star-gushing universe was usually obscured by them—the curtains and the murals—and Howard, by accident of birth, tasted the raw stuff of the cosmos. Other, larger, inhuman souls might very well thrive on such a feast. Howard thought angels, but the image he had of the seraphim, with their long blond curls and flowing white robes and golden halos, did not fit with the more frightening, dark, powerful species he conjured, which would gorge on and delight in what, when ingested by him, instead of sating, instantly burst the seams of his thin body. The aura, the sparkle and tingle of an oncoming fit, was not the lightning—it was the cooked air that the lightning pushed in front of itself. The actual seizure was when the bolt touched flesh, and in an instant so atomic, so nearly immaterial, nearly incorporeal, that there was almost no before and after, no cause A that led to effect B, but instead simply A, simply B, with no *then* in between, and Howard became pure, unconscious energy. It was like the opposite of death, or a bit of the same thing death was, but from a different direction: Instead of being emptied or extinguished to the point of unselfness, Howard was overfilled, overwhelmed to the same state. If death was to fall below some human boundary, so his seizures were to be rocketed beyond it.

Perhaps, Howard thought, the curtains and murals and pastel angels are a mercy, a dim reflection of things fit for the fragility of human beings. Whenever he looked at the angels in the family Bible, though, he saw their radiant golden halos and resplendent white robes and he shook with fear.

Ninety-six hours before he died, George said he wanted a shave. He was a fastidiously neat dresser. His jackets and shirts were always well tailored, if not made from the best cloth or in the latest fashion. Whiskers grew on his face in mangy patches; he could not have grown a beard or mustache had he ever wanted to. This made shaving all the more important to him. If he went a day without shaving, his babyish face, dotted with sparse stubble, lent him the look of an invalid or a large child incapable of taking care of his own needs.

Jesus, when was the last time I had a shave? How about a shave? He looked around the room at his family. There were his wife, his two daughters, Claire and Betsy, a smattering of grown-up grandchildren, and his one remaining sister, Marjorie, huffing for air, fitted with a thick neck collar for her latest case of whiplash. The collar was zipped into a sock of tan linen, which matched her pantsuit. Despite lifelong asthma, she smoked long ladies' cigarettes on the back porch, flicking the ash off with her thumb, her arms crossed, her breath coming in sibilant little puffs of blue smoke. She kept her package of cigarettes in a cloth case with a gold-colored clasp. The case was embroidered with tan beads set in fountaining water patterns. She heard her brother as she pitched her cigarette into the rhododendron bushes and came back into the room. The screen door slammed behind her, the bang impious in the dim funereal hush. (The morning George had gone to the hospital, feeling worse than usual, his plan for the day had been a trip to the hardware store to buy a new hydraulic arm for the door; the old arm no longer offered any resistance.)

Why hasn't anybody shaved Georgie? Who is going to shave Georgie? It's terrible. Georgie looks awful. My God, he looks *terrible*.

One of his grandsons, Samuel, said, Oh, Aunt Margie, you are right; we need to get this old goat looking presentable. I'll shave him. Say your prayers, Gramp, and keep still. He wanted to choke his great-aunt until she died and then smoke all of her cigarettes.

George said, I'm done for.

Sam said, Your turn in the barrel.

George said, I was in the barrel *last* night.

Sam came back into the room with a bowl of scalding water and a hot towel, shaving cream, and a cheap disposable plastic razor blade his grandmother had found for him in a basket beneath the bathroom sink that was filled with various disused, soap-crusted toiletry. He could not find his grandfather's electric razor and George could not remember where he had put it. No one had the presence of mind to run to the drugstore and buy a new razor. Sam pressed the hot towel to his grandfather's face and wished for a smoke and that he did not have to shave his grandfather in front of such a wrung-out, hysterical audience. George's head shook slightly from Parkinson's disease. The shaking stopped when Sam held George's face. Sam removed the towel and shook the can of shaving cream and pushed the dispenser button. The can was old, excavated along with the razor from the guts of the cabinet under the bathroom sink. Since George usually used an electric razor, he had no need for shaving cream. The can was rusty on the bottom and was a brand no longer even manufactured. The dispenser sputtered and sneezed a gob of white drool into Sam's hand.

Sam said, Never mind the wood, Mother.

George said, Father's coming home with a load.

Sam shook the can again and this time a dollop of something closer to actual shaving cream came out. Sam lathered George's face and neck. He began with George's cheeks, only shaving with the lay of the hair. The cheeks went smoothly. The upper lip was tougher, the lower tougher still.

Marjorie said, Don't *cut* him.

George's daughters grimaced. Betsy, Sam's mother, said, Be careful, and bared her teeth at Sam to express peril and worry and support.

George's wife, Sam's grandmother said, Get his chin; he always misses his chin.

Sam said, A smoke.

George said, What?

Sam said, Nothing. Keep still, Mr. Kresge.

Mr. Kresge, I got complaint, 'bout how you sell me this cheap red paint!

Then came George's wattle, the loose bag of skin between the underside of his chin and his neck, with short, light strokes. Sam pulled it tight this way and that and gingerly scraped the razor over George's soft skin. The effort drained Sam, and his craving for nicotine led him to shave in a haphazard manner. When he thought he was done and had wiped away the remains of the shaving cream from George's face, he saw that there was a patch of stubble left in a fold of neck skin. Instead of applying more hot water and cream, Sam said, Wait, missed a spot, and pulled the fold taut with his thumb and flicked at the patch with the razor. The razor caught skin and opened a cut.

Shit, said Sam.

George said, What?

Blood! said Marjorie.

The cut was not deep, but it bled impressively, sending a column of red down George's neck, which ran off into several tributaries as it reached various wrinkles and rolls, and stained the top of his white cotton johnny, making necessary the elaborate effort of getting George out of his stained bedclothes and into clean ones, a process more difficult than its simple mechanics because it involved daughters and grandchildren rolling George's blanched, helpless naked body from side to side. Marjorie had to be escorted from the room when this happened.

She saw his bared shoulders and chest and said, This is *awful!* Somebody *do* something! Tears welled in her eyes and she groaned.

George had not felt anything. Once the bleeding was stanched and a plastic bandage stuck over the cut, and George was in a new johnny, propped up in bed, Marjorie, along with the other more abashed of the family, returned to the room. Sam handed George a mirror. George looked surprised at his reflection, as if after a lifetime of seeing himself in mirrors and windows and metal and water, now, at the end, suddenly a rude, impatient stranger had shown up in place of himself, someone anxious to get into the picture, although his proper cue was George's exit.

This sent a fresh sense of alarm through the room, and Sam quickly said, Well, what do you think? George looked up, confused. Sam said, About the shave. George looked at his grandson, lost. Sam leaned his face very slightly forward toward his grandfather, holding his stare, and said again, in a quieter voice, What do you think about the shave?

George said, Oh! The *shave*, you say! Very, very good. I'm so pretty again.

Sam said, Like Little Leroy, the cabin boy.
George said, Ah, he was a *cautious* little nipper!

The rutted road ran between two mild slopes. The trees
that grew on the slopes leaned in toward the road, so
that their lowest branches brushed the grass. The sun
lowered and there was brightness in the treetops and
brightness in the long grass, and in between a band of
shadows gathered and held in the skirts of the lowest
branches. Howard rode along the track and had the
sense that once he passed, the shadows leaked out from
beneath the edge of the forest, down the incline and out
onto the dirt. Behind him also, along with the shadows,
animals came to browse in the grass at the verge, and a
black-booted red fox darted across the bright road, from
darkness to darkness. To Howard, this was the best part
of the afternoon, when folds of night mingled with
bands of day. He resisted the desire to stop the wagon
and give Prince Edward an apple and crawl into the
shadows and sit quietly and become a part of the slow
freshet of night, or to stop the wagon and simply remain
on the bench and watch the shadows approach and pool
around the wagon wheels and Prince Edward's hooves
and eventually reach the soles of his shoes and then his
ankles, until mule, cart, and man were submerged in
the flood tide of night, because the secrets gathered in
the shadows at the tree line that rustled and waited until he
passed, and which made the hair on his arms and the back

of his neck stand on end and his scalp tighten when he felt them flooding, invisible, the road around him, were dispelled each time he turned his direct attention to them, scattered to just beyond his sight. The true essence, the secret recipe of the forest and the light and the dark was far too fine and subtle to be observed *with my blunt eye—water sac and nerves, miracle itself, fine itself: light catcher. But the thing itself is not forest and light and dark, but something else scattered by my coarse gaze, by my dumb intention. The quilt of leaves and light and shadow and ruffling breezes might part and I'd be given a glimpse of what is on the other side; a stitch might work itself loose or be worked loose. The weaver might have made one bad loop in the foliage of a sugar maple by the road and that one loop of whatever the thread might be wound from—light, gravity, dark from stars—had somehow been worked loose by the wind in its constant worrying of white buds and green leaves and blood-and-orange leaves and bare branches and two of the pieces of whatever it is that this world is knit from had come loose from each other and there was maybe just a finger width's hole, which I was lucky enough to spot in the glitter-ing leaves from this wagon of drawers and nimble enough to scale the silver trunk and brave enough to poke my finger into the tear, that might offer to the simple touch a measure of tranquillity or reassurance.*

Such were the qualities of Howard's daydreams when Prince Edward pulled the cart with animal cer-tainty along the canopied dirt tracks and he fell into a

sort of waking stupor in which his mind was as it is
when a person sleeps but his dreams are composed by
his open eyes.

> *Crepuscule Borealis:* 1. The bark of birches glows sil-
> ver and white at dusk. The bark of birches peels like
> parchment. 2. Fireflies blink in the thick grass and
> form halos around hedges. 3. The spaces between
> the trees look like glowing coals. 4. Foxes keep to
> the shadows. Owls look down from branches. Mice
> make brisk collections.

Another incredible clock of which the author has had
the delight to hear is the clepsydra given by the king
of Persia to Charlemagne in 807.

Early man sought always methods of capturing
time more precisely than casting the shadows of
Apollo's chariot upon a graded iron disk (for when the
sun sank beneath the hills in the west, what then?), or
burning oil in a glass lamp marked at intervals so that
crude hours might be gleaned from the disappearing
fuel. The reasonable, sensitive soul who perhaps one
day while taking his rest along the banks of a bubbling
brook came to hear, in that half-dream, half-wakeful
state during which so many men seem most receptive
to perceiving the pulleys and winches that hoist the
clouds, the heavenly bellows that push the winds, the
cogs and wheels that turn the globe, came to hear a

regularity in the silvery song of water over pebbles, that soul is unknown to us. Let us remark, then, that it is good enough to induce him out of the profusions of the past, perhaps fit him with thick sandals and a steady hand, a heart open to nature and a head devoted to the advancement of men, and watch in admiration as he pokes and fiddles and persists at various machines until he arrives at a device which marks time by a steady flow of water through its guts. Let us name him, even: Ctesibius of Alexandria, and allow him the credit of constructing an engine which was the ancestor of that given by the Arab to Charles the Great to drip away the moments of his last seven years. First, a constant flow of water trickled from a reservoir into a receiving vessel. In the receiving vessel was a float fixed with a vertical rod. Perched on the top of the rod was a figure (we may imagine him with a turban and robe and a thick black beard and fierce black eyes). This figure held a pointer (again, we may imagine this pointer in the form of a lance or spear, which the warrior thrust at a ghostly adversary). The figure was raised as the water filled the vessel in which he was set. His pointer rose along the side of a column calibrated with twenty-four lines for the hours of the day. When the figure rose to the twenty-fourth line, the water in the vessel in which he floated reached a siphon. The siphon emptied the vessel and the figure sank back to the level of the first hour; that is, the mid of night.

The clock offered to Charlemagne had no such single figure, but rather a dial containing twelve doors. At the appropriate hour, the appropriate door would open and out would drop the appropriate number of small golden balls, which fell one at a time onto a brass drum fitted with a taut square of goat's hide. When the midnight hour had arrived and its twelve balls struck their twelve beats, twelve miniature horsemen rode forth and closed the twelve doors.

—from *The Reasonable Horologist*,
by the Rev. Kenner Davenport, 1783

George was dehydrated ninety-six hours before he died. The younger of his two daughters, Betsy, sat by the side of his bed, trying to give him water. The hospital had provided dozens of small, individually wrapped pink sponges on paper sticks. The sponges were meant to be dipped into water and then sucked on by patients too ill to drink from a cup. Betsy thought her father looked absurd, as if he were a baby sucking on a lollipop. She tried to get him to drink directly from the cup.

You must be so thirsty. Wouldn't you like a full sip instead of sucking on that awful sponge? She could not erase from her mind the image of her father sucking on a dirty kitchen sponge fetched from the bottom of a sink.

George said, Oh, that would be wonderful. Christ, I'm thirsty. When she held the cup to his lips and tilted it slightly, he looked at her and all of the water ran down his chin. When she soaked one of the sponges and stuck it in his mouth, he nearly swallowed it, stick and all. He choked and gagged. She pulled the sponge out and it was covered in thick white mucus.

That was good, he said. I'm so thirsty.

He was dying from renal failure. His actual death was going to be from poisoning by uric acid. Whatever food or water he managed to consume never came back out of his body.

Betsy said to her sister, her mother, and to her sons, He looks so thirsty. He needs water.

Her son Sam said, Thirsty is the least of his problems. Anyway, it's not like that anymore; he's *going to die*.

(The spring after he died and was buried in the local cemetery, Betsy planted red geraniums in front of his polished black headstone, which had the wrong date of his wife's birth carved on it. Which, his wife said, you can get fixed after I kick the bucket and they have to add *that* date. Betsy tended the geraniums until autumn. Every day after work, she put on her sneakers and walked the two miles from her house to the cemetery to talk to her father and water the flowers. There was a spigot and a plastic half-gallon milk container provided by the caretaker. She filled the container and poured it out at the base of the plants five times, until they stood in three inches of muddy water. Silvery streams ran from the grave through the green grass. Had the plot not been on the side of a hill, where the water quickly drained away, the flowers would have drowned within a week.)

Tempest Borealis: 1. The sky turned silver. The pond turned silver from the silver sky. It looked like a pool of mercury. The wind blew and the trees showed the silver-green undersides of their leaves. The sky turned from silver to green. We went to the dock where our wooden rowboats were tied by their noses to aluminum cleats. The wood of the dock was bleached silvery white. We knelt at the edge of the dock and leaned close to the water, so that the silver sky skin disappeared and we saw twigs and weeds and minnows and blood-plumped leeches squiggling along. We could not see them, but we knew that small silver-bellied brook trout hovered out of our view, several feet away, just under where the sky skin started again, beyond the ends of the boats. The trout were invisible in the water, green-backed like weeds and the green-black water grass, until they rolled over and broke the water skin to eat insects and showed their silver-green undersides. 2. Wind combed through the fir trees around the rim of the pond like a rumor, like the murmur of old men muttering about the storm behind the mountain. The storm came up from behind the mountain, shrouding the peak. Lightning crawled down the mountain and drank at the water, lapped the shallows with electric tongues, stunning bolt-eyed frogs and small trout and silver minnows. Thunder cracked like falling timber and shook the cabin as it clapped the water skin.

A late-spring storm capped the last daffodils and the first tulips with dollops of snow, which melted when the sun came back out. The snow seemed to have a bracing effect on the flowers; their roots drank the cold melt, their stalks straightened from the chilly drink; their petals, supple and hale, were spared the brittle coating of a true freeze. The afternoon became warm, and with the warmth the first bees appeared, and each little bee settled in a yellow cup and took suck like a newborn. Howard stopped Prince Edward, even though he was behind in his rounds, and gave the mule a carrot and stepped into the field full of flowers and bees, who seemed not to mind his presence in the least, who seemed, in fact, in their spring thrall, to be unaware of his presence at all. Howard closed his eyes and inhaled. He smelled cold water and cold, intrepid green. Those early flowers smelled like cold water. Their fragrance was not the still perfume of high summer; it was the mineral smell of cold, raw green. He crouched to look at a daffodil. Its six-petaled corona was fully unfurled, like a bright miniature sun. A bee crawled in its cup, massaging stigma and anther and style. Howard leaned as closely as he dared (he imagined sniffing the poor bee into his nose, the subsequent sting, the unfortunate wound, the plucked and dead creature on its back in the flattened, cold grass) and inhaled again. There was a faint sweetness mingled with the sharp mineral cold, which faded from detection when he inhaled more deeply in order to smell it better.

The field was an abandoned lot. The remnants of an old house, long since fallen into ruin, stood at the back of the field. The flowers must have been the latest generation of perennials, whose ancestors were first planted by a woman who lived in the ruins when the ruins were a raw, unpainted house inhabited by herself and a smoky, serious husband and perhaps a pair of silent, serious daughters, and the flowers were an act of resistance against the raw, bare lot with its raw house sticking up from the raw earth like an act of sheer, inevitable, necessary madness because human beings have to live somewhere and in something and here is just as outrageous as there because in either place (in any place) it seems like an interruption, an intrusion on something that, no matter how many times she read in her Bible, Let them have dominion, seemed marred, dispelled, vanquished once people arrived with their catastrophic voices and saws and plows and began to sing and hammer and carve and erect. So the flowers were maybe a balm or, if not a balm, some sort of gesture signifying the balm she would apply were it in her power to offer redress. The flowers Howard now walked among were the few last heirs to that brief local span of disaster and regeneration and he felt close to the sort of secrets he often caught himself wondering about, the revelations of which he only ever realized he had been in the proximity of after he became conscious of that proximity, and that phe-nomenon, of becoming conscious, was the very thing that whisked him away, so that any bit of insight or gleaning was available only in retrospect, as a sort of afterglow that remained but that was not accessible through words. He thought, But what about through grass and flowers and light and shadow?

Howard opened a drawer in his wagon and took a box of pins, which he wrote off in his inventory book and paid for out of his own pocket with two dull pen-nies. He lashed four sticks together with blades of grass. Then he selected more blades of grass, according to their breadth. These he lay across the square frame and fixed to the twigs with the pins. He stretched the first blades too tautly and the grass tore on the pins. Eventually, he found the right pressure, the amount of tug the grass could withstand before it tore along its grain against the column of the pin. He impaled the blades in an alternating order, one laid stalk to tip, left to right, the next laid tip to stalk, so that the grass made a seamless panel of green over the square. When he fin-ished tacking the last blade to the frame, Howard opened another drawer in the wagon and took out a pair of sewing scissors. The scissors came in a brown cardboard box with a drawing of them cutting cloth from a bolt. They were wrapped in a square of stiff, cloudy white paper. Howard carefully unrolled them from the paper and trimmed the grass so that it conformed to the boundaries of the square. He cut with just the tips of the scissors' blades, and when he finished, he rubbed the blades clean with the cuff of his shirt (leaving arrowhead-shaped stains of grass green) and wrapped the scissors back in their paper and put them back in their box and put the box back in its proper drawer. He held the object to the wind, hoping for a note. He held the object to the sun and the green lit up in a bright panel.

Wildflowers dotted the field along with the perennials. Howard collected buttercups (*habitat: old fields, meadows, disturbed areas*) and small white blossoms that trembled in the breeze, and which he could not name. These he wove by their stalks into his warp of grass, alternating the yellow flowers with the white. He threaded one hundred blossoms. Deer came to graze in the long shadows. When he looked up, the day had nearly passed. He had neglected his rounds. The only money he had in his box was the two pennies he had taken from his own pocket for the pins. Cullen, his agent, owned all of one of them and nearly all of the other. Howard considered shaving off the sliver of penny, as slight as a fingernail clipping, the convex angle dull and dirty, the concave bright and clean, and returning home to Kathleen and dropping the sliver into her open hand. He considered her surprise and her usual anger and then that anger turning back to surprise and then into delight as he took his tapestry of grass and flowers from behind his back and put it in her hands. She would look at it this way and that, holding it between herself and an oil lamp, the same way that he had with the sun, to see the light illuminate the living green. She would bring the panel to her face and smell the flowers and the bruised stalks. She would hold the panel beneath her upturned chin and ask if he could see the reflections from the buttercups and laugh. She would say, These white ones are called windflowers.

Howard shivered, suddenly cold. Summer would anneal the chilled earth, but for now the water was so mineral and hard that it seemed to ring. Howard heard the water reverberating through the soil and around the roots. Water lay ankle-deep amid the grass. Puddles wobbled and the light cast on them through the clouds shimmered and they looked like tin cymbals. They looked as if they would ring if tapped with a stick. The puddles rang. The water rang. Howard dropped his tapestry of grass and flowers. The buzzing bees joined into one ringing chord that pulsed. The field rang and spun.

Eighty-four hours before he died, George thought, Because they are like tiles loose in a frame, with just enough space so they can all keep moving around, even if it's only a few at a time and in one place, so that it doesn't seem like they are moving, but the empty space between them, and that empty space is the space that is missing, the last several pieces of colored glass, and when those pieces are in place, that will be the final picture the final arrangement. But those pieces, smooth and glossy and lacquered, are the dark tablets of my death, in gray and black, and bleached, drained, and until they are in place, everything else will keep on shifting. And so this end in confusion, where when things stop I never get to know it, and this moving is that space, is that what is yet to be, which is for others to see filled wherever it may finally be in the frame when the last pieces are fitted and the others stop, and there will be the stopped pattern, the final array, but not even that, because that final finitude will itself be a bit of scrolling, a pearlescent clump of tiles, which will generally stay together but move about within another whole and be mingled with in endless ways of other people's memories, so that I will remain a set of impressions porous and open to combination with all of the other vitreous squares floating about in whoever else's frames, because there is always the space left in reserve for the rest of their own time, and to my great-grandchildren, with more space than tiles, I will be no more than the smoky arrangement of a set of rumors, and to their great-grandchildren I will be no more than a tint of some obscure color, and to their great grandchildren nothing they ever know about, and so what army of strangers and ghosts has shaped and colored me until back to Adam, until back to when ribs were blown from molten sand into the glass bits that took up the light of this world because they were made from this world, even though the fleeting tenants of those bits of colored glass have vacated them before they have had even the remotest understanding of what it is to inhabit them, and if they—if we are fortunate (yes, I am lucky, lucky), and if we are fortunate, have fleeting instants when we are satisfied that the mystery is ours to ponder, if never to solve, or even just rife personal mysteries, never mind those outside—are there even mysteries outside? a puzzle itself—but anyway, personal mysteries, like where is my father, why can't I stop all the moving and look out over the vast arrangements and find by the contours and colors and qualities of light where my father is, not to solve anything but just simply even to see it again one last time, before what, before it ends, before it stops. But it doesn't stop; it simply ends. It is a final pattern scattered without so much as a pause at the end, at the end of what, at the end of this.

Howard stood in the darkened doorway, cold, wet, and muddy. It was nine o'clock—four hours after dinnertime and one hour after the bedtime of his daughters, Darla and Marjorie, and his younger son, Joe. The bedtime of his elder son, George, was right around now because of his job after school and his nighttime chores (which included getting his brother ready for bed because his brother was ten but had the mind of a three-year-old) and his homework. The family was sitting around the dining room table, the two girls on one side, the two boys on the other, his wife, Kathleen, at the far end, and his own chair empty, with a plateful of cold food in front of it. There were platefuls of cold food in front of all of the children and his wife. Confused and exhausted, his first thought when he saw them was, The children must be nearly hysterical. He did not know what time it was except that it was late, and for the second time that day he had the sensation of being in the middle of some sort of overlap, as if he, wrecked and half-frozen and bloodied, had brought night into the dining room and mixed up his family's eating at the proper hour with his own afflicted time. He could not quite sort out the vision, as if he had stumbled into some other world where it was perfectly normal to have the family dinner at nine o'clock. Kathleen looked at him. She said nothing. Howard was not sure if she expected him to come into the room, trailing a wake of mud, and sit at the table and bow his head and say grace as he always did—Let us rejoice that there is nothing better—and then pick up knife and fork and begin to eat the cold, coagulated servings of food as if they were hot and he was not soiled and cut and soaked and it was not nine o'clock at night and the world was as it should be instead of as it was.

Joe took his thumb from his mouth and said, Daddy's muddy!

Darla stared at her father and said, Mummy, Mummy, Mummy!

Marjorie wheezed and said, Father. You. Are. *Filthy*!

Joe said, Daddy's muddy! Daddy's muddy!

Darla stared at the darkened doorway where Howard stood, saying, Mummy, Mummy, Mummy, each time a little louder, each time a bit more shrilly, even after Kathleen looked at the children and, without saying a word, told them to sit right where they were and then stood and took him to the laundry room to get him dry clothes and to scrub the mud from his face and hands with a facecloth.

George stood and went to Joe and said, That's right, Joe, Daddy's muddy, but Mummy's cleaning him up and then we can finally eat. George gave Joe his blanket, which the boy had dropped to the floor in his excitement.

Joe put a corner of the blanket up his nose and his thumb back in his mouth, but continued to say, 'ally's mully, while he held his thumb between his teeth.

George went to Darla and dipped her napkin in her drinking water and dabbed it on her forehead and said, It's okay, Darla, it's okay, until she calmed somewhat.

Mummy has to do something, Mummy has to do something, she whispered. Marjorie's asthma made her whistle when she breathed and her voice came out a squeak. Well, she said, gasping, I am—she collected a breath, another, another, to save enough air for the word—*eating*. She reached for the long-since-cold mashed potatoes. When she lifted the bowl, she was too weak and plunked it back down and dropped back into her chair. George turned her chair out from the table and helped her get to her feet.

He said, You need to get in bed. I'll get your vapor cloths and your asthma powder. Don't worry what Mummy says. I'll bring you up some chicken and potatoes.

Kathleen cleaned Howard in the laundry room. Howard sat, silent, testing his badly bitten tongue on the roof of his mouth. Kathleen scrubbed his face until his cheeks went raw and shone nearly as red as the blood she had just washed off. Howard said, I remember my mother doing this for me the first time it happened. Kathleen buttoned the clean shirt she'd put on him and said, Now you can go eat your dinner with your family.

By the time they had eaten and cleared the table and changed for bed, it was quarter after ten. Kathleen never acted as if anything were wrong. She ignored the four-hour gap during which she had made her litter sit before their plates and wait for Howard. When he came into the driveway slumped in the cart, Prince Edward pulling, slow but certain, and staggered through the door, she took up with the evening again as if it were five in the afternoon, as if she had just slid the five o'clock hour to the nine o'clock one, or took the four hours between them and banished them or tyrannized herself and her children into a type of abatement, leaving each of them and herself with a burden of four extra hours that each would have to juggle and mind for the rest of their lives, first as a single, strange, indigestible puzzlement and then later as a prelude to the night nearly a year later when she and the children again sat in front of full plates of cold food, waiting for Howard, waiting for the sounds of the cart and the mule and the jangling tack, and that time he never came back at all.

Once the girls and Joe were in bed and the kitchen was cleaned and Kathleen was in the bedroom changing into her nightdress, Howard, still numbed, still crackling with the voltage of his seizure, stopped George as the boy was putting his and his sisters' books away and said, George, I. . . . And George said, It's all right, although it wasn't, and because his mother and father managed to hide from the children the spectacle of an actual fit and to act as if the epilepsy did not even exist, the rumors of the illness, the odd euphemisms and elliptical silences were more terrifying than the condition they meant to obscure. And then George went off to bed. Howard shuffled through the dark house to the Franklin stove in the parlor, which, because he was still so cold, he over-stoked with birch logs before he finally went to bed.

Howard and Kathleen and the children all woke at the same time, just before dawn, drenched in sweat. They all shuffled into the parlor at the same time, like sleepwalkers, to find the iron stove glowing white with heat and pulsing like a hot coal.

2

THE MORNINGS BEGAN IN THE DARK. THEY began with setting the home in order for the day, so that it might already be industrious when the sun climbed first the invisible horizon and then the branches of the dark trees.

Fill the stove box with wood. Fill the milk pail with milk. (How that pail clanking against George's leg as he crosses the yard splits the seamless night, wakes the other children, who sniffle and yawn and root deeper into their warm beds, dreading the cold air and morning chores. Mother will find Marjorie sitting up in bed and wheezing. Darla will open her eyes and say, The sun's late. The sun's late! I'm sure it was up earlier yesterday! Mummy! Something's wrong! Joe will be found with a foot in the wrong leg of his overalls, grinning and asking for pancakes and maple syrup, his favorite meal.) Fetch the water. Make a fire.

Your cold mornings are filled with the heartache about the fact that although we are not at ease in this world, it is all we have, that it is ours but that it is full of strife, so that all we can call our own is strife; but even that is better than nothing at all, isn't it? And as you split frost-laced wood with numb hands, rejoice that your uncertainty is God's will and His grace toward you and that *that* is beautiful, and part of a greater certainty, as your own father always said in his sermons and to you at home. And as the ax bites into the wood, be comforted in the fact that the ache in your heart and the confusion in your soul means that you are still alive, still human, and still open to the beauty of the world, even though you have done nothing to deserve it. And when you resent the ache in your heart, remember: You will be dead and buried soon enough.

Howard resented the ache in his heart. He resented that it was there every morning when he woke up, that it remained at least until he had dressed and had some hot coffee, if not until he had taken stock of the goods in his brush cart, and fed and hitched Prince Edward, if not until his rounds were done, if not until he fell asleep that night, and if his dreams were not tormented by it. He resented equally the ache and the resentment itself. He resented his resentment because it was a sign of his own limitations of spirit and humility, no matter that he understood that such was each man's burden. He resented the ache because it was uninvited, seemed imposed, a sentence, and, despite the encouragement he gave himself each morning, it baffled him because it was there whether the day was good or bad, whether he witnessed major kindness or minor transgression, suffered sourceless grief or spontaneous joy.

This morning—the Monday morning after the Friday morning when there was predawn snow and Howard had stopped to look at a field that had once been a homestead and had, in a fugue state, made a contraption out of twigs and grass and flowers, which he had already forgotten making, and then had had a seizure and awoke freezing in the field and had finally realized who he was and where he was and had made his way home—this morning brought fear that there hid somewhere on one of the back roads that he intended to canvass another seizure, a bolt of lightning coiled behind a rock or stump or within the hollow of a tree or some strange nest and which his passing would trigger to spring, to explode, and to impale him.

Such vanity! What gall to elect for yourself such attention, good or bad. Project yourself above yourself. Look at the top of your dusty hat: cheap felt, wilted and patched with scraps from the last wilted and patched felt hat. What a crown! What a king you are to deserve such displeasure, how important that God stop whatever it is He is tending and pitch bolts at your head. Rise higher, above the trees. Your crown is already hard to see amid the dust of the road and dirt of the ditch. But you are still remarkable. Rise higher, perhaps to the height where the blackbirds flap. Where have you gone? Oh, there you are, I think. That is you, isn't it, that wisp inching along? Well, rise higher, then, to the belly of the clouds. Where have you gone? Now higher, to where, if you are not careful, you might stub your toe on the mountains of the moon. Where are you? Never mind you; where is your home, your county, your state, your nation? Ah, there it is! And higher now, so that your hair and the lashes of your eyes catch fire from the sparks of solar flares. On which of those bright bodies do you rule your kingdom of dirt, your cart of soap? Very well, that one. I hope you are right—there is little need for a tinker on Mars. Now higher again, past the eighth planet, named for the king of the sea. And higher again, past the shadowy ninth, which for now only exists in the dreams of men back on— Well! Where have you gone? Which among those millions of glittering facets is where you belong? Where is it you toil and drum and fall to the ground and thrash in the weeds?

The weather turned warm and on Sundays after church the family sat on the porch. The porch ran the length of the front of the house and was surrounded by a thick collar of wildflowers. In early July, there was Queen Anne's lace and columbines, hawkweed and forget-me-nots, black-eyed Susans and bluebells. There was a bank of loosestrife in the crabgrass and clover across the lawn, between the porch and the verge of the road. The floor of the porch was uneven and ran at a slight incline from one end (where the front door was) to the other (just past the window, through which the dining room table was visible). Looked at from the road, the house appeared to lean toward the left and the porch to the right, so that it appeared the only thing keeping either standing was their mutual pull on each other. From the side of the house, though, it seemed that the opposite was true, that they slumped against one another and remained upright by virtue of their mutual weight. Viewed from whatever angle, the homestead had the look of claptrap. The walls all seemed as if they were about to fall over, one upon the next, and the sagging roof to drop on top of the pile, so that the flattened house would make a neat stacked deck.

The porch was unpainted and its wood bleached to a silvery white. When the sky filled with clouds, it often turned the same silver color as the wood, so that it only seemed missing a grain to be wood and the wood only missing a breath of wind to stir it and turn it into sky. There was a spot on the floor, just to the right of the front door, which, when walked on, made the whole porch bob as if it rested on a branch. There were two decrepit chairs, one an old rocking chair, which had once been painted red, and in which Kathleen sat and shelled peas or snapped beans and barked, Get where I can see you, at Joe, who was rolling around in the side lot. Howard sat in the other chair. It was old, with a ladder back, which made a parallelogram with the floor and listed to one side or the other, according to how Howard sat on it, and the back of which came apart at the splats, so that he had to stand every couple of minutes and clap the piece of furniture back together. The children sat on upended buckets or on packing crates. Buddy the Dog and Russell the Cat lay on patches of sun. Darla and Marjorie helped Kathleen: Marjorie when she was not upstairs in bed, suffering from an asthma attack brought on by pollen and ragweed, and Darla when she did not see a wasp or spider which, sooner or later, she always did, and which sent her shrieking back into the house, as often as not over the springy part of the floor, so that the rest of the family was left to steady themselves on the swaying porch as she fled to the hollow depths of the house. Howard and George played cribbage.

Seven.

Fifteen for two.

Twenty-four for three.

Thirty for four.

Go.

Thirty-one for two.

They played without a board and kept score by adding their points in the margins of the comics pages from the newspaper. *Father said, George, I can't find the cribbage board, and I said, That's funny, Daddy; it should be on the porch, where we left it. I pretended to help him look for it for an hour until he gave up and I pretended to and we used a piece of old newspaper to keep score. I took the board. I stole it and took it to Ray's shed, where we smoked and played cribbage for marbles or an arrowhead.*

You missed a fifteen, and the right jack is three more.

So it is. You got me again, George.

I smell a skunk, a double skunk.

Kathleen said, George, go get your brother. Go get him.

No looking.

I won't. George got off the crate.

Walk. So he walked. He turned the corner of the house and called for his brother and when he saw him, stuck in a tree and gnawing on a handful of flowers, he picked up a pebble and threw it at him. The stone struck Joe on the ear and he began to cry. George said, loudly enough for his mother and father to hear around the corner, O, Joe, don't cry. I'll get you out of there. Joe, don't cry. I'll get you some water to wash out the bitter taste of starflowers and daisies.

What of miniature boats constructed of birch bark and fallen leaves, launched onto cold water clear as air? How many fleets were pushed out toward the middles of ponds or sent down autumn brooks, holding treasures of acorns, or black feathers, or a puzzled mantis?

Let those grassy crafts be listed alongside the iron hulls that cleave the sea, for they are all improvisations built from the daydreams of men, and all will perish, whether from ocean siege or October breeze.

And what of barges made to burn? One evening at sunset, as he was walking through the woods near the house after dinner, Howard caught sight of George kneeling on a path, examining something on the ground. George did not hear him, so Howard stood quietly in the trees and watched his son. George rose and hurried back up the path toward the house. He ran out of Howard's view and a moment later the door to the front porch slapped shut. Howard went to where his son had knelt and found a dead mouse, curled as if sleeping, on the leaves. It had not been dead for long. Its head went back and its limbs opened up when Howard toed it with his boot, after which it curled back up again. The porch door swung shut again and Howard stepped back into the shadows in the trees.

George returned to the mouse and wrapped it in newspaper and bound the shroud tightly with kitchen string. He stuffed the wrapped mouse into an empty box of kitchen matches. Howard smelled kerosene and understood that his son had soaked the newspaper with it.

There was a small pond through the woods behind the yard. It was a stopping place for two pairs of ducks and a small flock of Canada geese every year. Its depth was no more than five feet at its deepest. Sometimes,

George fished there and caught small brook trout, which he cooked over a fire he made at the edge of the water. If it was a Saturday, he fished at sundown, when, during the early summer, there were mayfly and drake hatches that brought the trout up to the surface to feed. At some point, bats would flit from the darkness out over the water to feed on the insects. George would stop fishing then, because the bats struck at his fishing fly and he had terrible notions of a frantic squeaking bat impaled on the barbed hook, trying to free itself and only breaking its own fragile wings in the process. Grabbing the bat and yanking the hook out would be unthinkable, so the only choice seemed as if it would be to run away, leaving the struggling animal on the end of the line, and to return the next morning to collect the rod and hope that a fox had happened along and eaten the bat (and not swallowed the hook along with the bat, so that it, too, now struggled somewhere in the woods, dragging the fishing pole by the taut line that now ran from its gut up through its throat and tore at the side of its mouth). So, when the bats came out, George cooked what fish he had, if he had any, and watched darkness settle and then went home.

George walked to the water and Howard followed silently behind at a distance. At the edge of the water, George cut a panel of bark from a birch tree with his jack-knife. He sewed the bark together at each end with a heavy sewing needle and dark thread, making a canoe-shaped boat. He placed the tiny coffin in the middle of the craft and laid a piece of coal, which he took from a pocket in his overalls, next to it. He lit the coal with a kitchen match, which he struck on his zipper fly, and launched the boat. It floated out onto the pond. The burning coal illuminated the birch bark and made it look like some sort of glowing animal hide. The air was still and the surface of the pond was sleek and reflective, like oil, and seemed thick, like oil, too, because the ripples trailing off the back of the little boat spread so slowly, as if the skin of the water offered more resistance against the influence of bodies passing through it that night. White moths came up from the grass at the pond's edge and fluttered out to the boat to flirt with the fire. The fire reached the matchbox and rubbed at it until it began to smoke. When the fire reached inside the box and touched the kerosene-soaked shroud, there was a bright, quiet thump and the bier was gulped in flame. The birch crackled and spat sparks. Then there was a gout of whitish smoke, which Howard imagined was the mouse burning. George's silhouette lit up against the flames on the water. The pyre sank with a hiss and a final spurt of smoke and the pond went dark and was quiet again.

Cremation came to Howard's mind, a vision of Viking kings lying on their funeral beds on the decks of their dragon-prow ships, swords in hand, set alight, and sent blazing into the dark surf, flames snapping from the ships' sterns like pennants in a gale.

Howard felt the movement of his son passing him in the dark more than he saw him, and he waited, listening, for the boy to make his way through the trees, up the path, back to the yard, and into the house before he himself went on, not to the house but past it, up to the road, and then turned back around, so that if anyone in the house saw, it would look as if he was returning from the after-dinner walk he had said he was taking. He came to the front of the house and could see George and Darla and Marjorie through the front window at the dining room table doing their homework.

I will pay my debts with honey!

What if the wagon, instead of a house on wheels, contained a kingdom of bees? There would be a panel on one side, fixed at the top with brass hinges, which would open and be propped up with poles at the corners. There would be windows looking into the hives. People could stand and watch the bees work while I gave lectures on the insects' habits, their industry and their loyalty. I could charge two cents a person. Young children could see the hives for free. Schools could send entire classes, or, even better, I could go to the schools and set up right in the yards. I could plant a bed of flowers on top of the wagon for the pollen and put the entrances to the hives on the side opposite the windows, so that the spectators would not bother the bees. And I could have a cabinet built into the back of

the wagon that I would fill with jars of honey and
beeswax and honeycombs tied with bright ribbons,
which I would sell to the audience after the lecture. I
could have a sign painted across the side panel: "The
Magnificent Cros-bees!"

Instead, winter came and he put the wagon away in
the barn, where mice and stray cats nested in a half-
frozen truce in the drawers.

George experienced all but one of his father's seizures as
rumors. He would find his mother leaning over his
rumpled, shaken father in a chair. There was spit in his
father's hair and blood on his chin. His father sat, snort-
ing rapid breaths through his nose and looking first at the
palms of his hands and then at their backs as he clenched
and unclenched them the way a soldier might after a bomb
had detonated in his trench and he was shocked to find
himself still alive and possibly unharmed. George came to
understand that this was because his father could tell
when the fits were coming and always managed, with the
help of George's mother, to get to a part of the house or
yard where the children were absent, so that they would
not have to see him in the throes of a seizure. If one of
the children happened along, Kathleen would say in a
flat, quite voice, You just go right back where you came
from; Father and I are busy. The one time he and his
brother and his sisters had watched their father have a
grand mal seizure was at Christmas dinner, 1926.

The children were astonished by the ham that Kathleen had cooked for the Christmas meal. It was the largest they had ever seen. It was covered in a crust of brown sugar and molasses. Buddy the Dog sat at attention, as if recommending himself to the ham over the children by his proper manners. Kathleen shooed him with a kick in the ribs, but he just let out a yelp and stayed put. Russell the Cat came into the room, too, and sat facing the wall, away from the table, cleaning his paws, as if an affectation of utter disinterest might be the trick to getting a scrap.

Howard had specially sharpened the carving knife for the occasion. He stood and leaned over the ham and, grinning at the children and at his wife, who scowled and told George to get his brother set in his chair and the girls that they'd get the spoon across the backs of their legs if they didn't sit their backsides down. Howard sliced into the ham, releasing even more of its sweet fragrance into the room, which nearly mesmerized everyone, Kathleen included. Her frown disappeared and even she had to stare at the ham for a moment in admiration. After Howard had carved two slices, however, she regained her usual composure and began directing the children to offer their plates to their father for their portions.

George, get Jack his ham and cut it for him. No, smaller pieces; he'll try to swallow those whole and choke himself. Darla, stop that silliness. Take some beans and pass them on. Howard, cut the slices thinner; this has to last us the week, since you saw fit to take a ham instead of the money you are owed to provide properly for your family.

Howard lifted a daub of potato with his fork. Then he speared two string beans and then a piece of ham. He raised the food to his mouth but stopped before he took the bite. The muscles at the hinges of his jaws flexed. He gasped. His eyelids fluttered. His eyes rolled in their sockets. The fork and food dropped from his hand and clattered onto his plate.

Mummy, what's—,

Howard scrambled his legs, trying to get up, but he only twisted around in his chair, which corkscrewed out from under him. He dropped to the floor, striking his head on the seat of the chair next to him as he fell.

Kathleen barked at Margie, Get your brother out of here, and seemed to shove her three youngest children, who had already huddled together in a trembling knot near the door, out of the room with a single shove. She rounded the corner of the table and stuck her hand out at George, who still sat at his seat, dumbly holding a fork straight up in the air, his mouth wide open.

George, give me the spoon. George looked at his mother. George, the spoon, she said, not angry or loud or bitter, as usual, but almost gently. He dropped his fork and yanked the spoon out of the potatoes.

He said, There's still—

Kathleen said, Give me the *spoon*, George. She snatched the spoon from George's hand and pounced on her husband, straddling his chest. Howard grunted and Kathleen jammed the spoon crosswise into his mouth, like a bit, so that he would not bite his own tongue off. Howard bit down onto the spoon and George watched as his father's lips curled back from his teeth, thinking, Like a skull's, not a man's, not Daddy's.

George, get here and hold the spoon. Like this. George was terrified of sitting on his father's chest.

Use two hands. Lean on it. Don't let his head bang. George felt his father's body quaking beneath him and was sure that it was going to rend itself apart, that his father was going to split open.

Mum.

I'm getting a stick. Kathleen ran out of the room and George heard her crash into the kitchen table, sending pots and pans clattering across the floor. She groaned and came back with a fresh piece of the kindling George had split that morning. Just as she reached George and Howard, the spoon handle split in Howard's mouth and George fell forward onto his father's face. George tried to catch himself, but his hands slid on a pool of greasy, dark blood collecting on the floor under his father's head. He pushed himself back up with the heels of his hands and saw that his father had opened his mouth and that he was about to swallow half of the spoon handle. George stuck his fingers into

Howard's mouth to get the spoon and Howard bit down onto them. George gasped. He saw his fingers clenched in his father's bloody teeth.

Kathleen spoke in a low monotone. It's okay, Georgie. It's okay. Can you hold the stick? Hold the stick. She began to try to pry Howard's mouth open. Let me get his chin, Georgie. She grabbed her husband's mouth as if it were a sprung bear trap.

What if she breaks Daddy's mouth? George thought.

Get the stick in, Georgie—the end. Get it in. Work it in. Howard's head banged the floor and banged the floor and banged the floor again. George managed to wedge the end of the stick in between his father's teeth at the side of his mouth. Kathleen instantly took the stick and ferociously worked it deeper. Without looking, she grabbed a seat cushion from the floor and slid it under her husband's head in between bangs on the floor. Howard's feet kicked at the legs of the table. Darla stood in the doorway and shrieked. Margie gasped for breath. Joe squealed.

Daddy's broken!

That's it, Georgie; that's almost it, little lamb.

There was so much noise from my father's boots kicking the floor and kicking the legs of the table, so that everything on it jumped and crashed back down or leapt off the table and clattered or shattered on the floor. Glass and food and forks and knives were all over the floor and Buddy the Dog whined and barked and Joe and Darla screamed but my father was in the middle of it, strangely quiet, as if concentrating or distracted, as wires and springs and ribs and guts popped and exploded and unraveled and unhinged. He was smiling when he nearly bit my fingers off, or it felt like he did and that was quiet, too. My mother got hold of his chin and I forced the cedar stick into those bloody teeth, and I didn't feel like I might be hurting a person anymore, which made me sicker. And there was blood everywhere from my fingers, which seemed detached from my hand and just to dangle from it, although I could feel blood thumping in them. And there was blood all over my father's face and in his mouth, which was my blood, and in his hair and on the floor, which was his blood from the cut he got on his head when it hit the chair as he fell. And for some reason, I noticed Russell the Cat bobbing his head, with his ears pricked up and his eyes wide and his pupils contracted and his little triangle nose twitching as he sniffed and stared at the blood. Instead of terror, though, I thought, So, this is what it is; I know what it is now. My father is not a werewolf or a bear or a monster and now I can run away.

And here is Kathleen, lying in her bed, which is set in the bare branches of a tree as dark as a burned-out vision—black-limbed, ash-sapped, spun in night. It is winter and winter winds shake the branches and the bed moves with them. It is winter, and the tree has been stripped of its bright mantle of leaves. It is winter because she lies awake with a bare heart, trying to remember a fuller season. She thinks, I must have been a young woman once.

She lies on one half of the bed. The dark form of her sleeping husband lies on the other half, turned away, sleeping so deeply, it is as if sleep is another world. Only her face is visible above the top of the bedcovers. It glows like a pale egg. Beneath her face, tucked under her chin, is the clean, ironed, starched white sheet, folded back over the top quilt evenly and overlapping it by exactly six inches, as her mother taught her when she was a young girl. Her hair is pinned up and covered by a sleeping cap that her mother sewed for her many years ago. Although her hair reaches below her waist, she lets it down only to wash it—twice a month in summer, once a month in winter. Her hair is auburn but has lost its richness; it has begun to thin on the crown of her head. She finds herself furious that the cut on her husband's head might bleed through the bandages and stain the clean pillowcase. She hears George groan in his sleep in his room across the hall. None of his fingers seem broken, but he probably needs a stitch or two to properly close the wounds made by Howard's teeth. She could not raise Dr. Box on the phone, since it was Christmas Day, so she plans to take George to his office first thing in the morning.

Her stern manner and her humorless regime mask bitterness far deeper than any of her children or her husband imagine. She has never recovered from the

shock of becoming a wife and then a mother. She is
still dismayed every morning when she first sees her
children, peaceful, sleeping, in their beds when she
goes to wake them, that as often as not the feeling she
has is one of resentment, of loss. These feelings frighten
her so much that she has buried them under layer
upon layer of domestic strictness. She has managed, in
the dozen years since becoming a wife and mother, to
half-convince herself that this nearly martial ordering
of her household is, in fact, the love that she is so terrified that she does not have. When one of her children wakes with a fever and a painful cough early one
freezing January morning, instead of kissing the child's
forehead and tucking him or her in more snugly and
boiling water for a mug of honey and lemon water,
she says that it is not man's lot to be at ease in this
world and that if she took a day off every time she had
a sniffle or a stiff neck, the house would unravel
around them all and they would be like birds with no
nest, so get up and get dressed and help your brother
with the wood, your sister with the water, and yanks
the covers off of the shivering child and throws its
cold clothes at it and says, Go get dressed, unless you
want a good dousing. She has convinced herself, at
least in the light of day, that this is love, that this is the
best way she can raise her children to be strong. She
could not live with herself if she allowed herself to
believe that she treated her own this way because she

felt no more connected to them than she would to a collection of stones.

As she falls asleep, half-dreaming of flight and beds in trees, she decides that it is time to do something about her sick husband. She will ask about it after Dr. Box has looked at George's hand.

The next morning, she dressed early. There was a frost on the inside of the windows and no sight of the sun yet.

Howard stirred and asked, What's that?

Kathleen said, I'm taking George to the doctor.

What for? What? Howard said.

Kathleen answered, For his bite, Howard; for the bite you gave him.

Howard croaked, The bite? A bite?

The walk to Dr. Box's house, the front two rooms of the first floor of which served as his office, was a little over two miles. Dawn overtook Kathleen and George as they walked along the side of the road, she in front and he shuffling behind her, half-asleep and only aware of the cold and his aching hand. At first, it was just a cindery lightening of night, then a red light beyond the horizon that illuminated the undersides of clouds coming from the west. Kathleen had worried that she might lose her resolve to speak with Dr. Box about her husband, but as she and George came closer to his office, her determination grew.

Dr. Box's house was tucked into the last bend in the road before entering West Cove. Kathleen and George came over a low slope, expecting to see the two-story building with its wraparound porch, where patients who were not too ill or sometimes not ill at all liked to sit in the summer and gossip as they waited for a tincture to cure their sour stomachs or a poultice to spread over a throbbing corn.

The house was gone. Kathleen stopped walking and looked around. The clouds that had colored the dawn copper had advanced and were now fastened overhead like a lid of stone. Flurries of snow spun in the wind. Kathleen surely stood in the right place and the doctor's house surely was vanished. Instead of the house, there was a hole in the earth. What had been Dr. Box's storage cellar, where his bottles of ether and rolls of bandages had stood alongside jars of pickled cucumbers and tomatoes and pears in syrup, was now an empty ditch exposed to the elements, already filling with snow and the windblown detritus of winter.

What happened, Mum? Was there a tornado?

A trail of fresh earth and deep ruts led from what had been Dr. Box's front yard out to the road and continued around the bend toward West Cove. Kathleen stood at the verge of the foundation. Without the house in its proper place, the lake beyond the trees in the former backyard was visible. Kathleen turned back to the road, and then back to the hole in the earth, unsure of what to do. A panic fluttered in her that all of West Cove might be gone, that if she walked beyond the bend in the road, she would find a bare, raw clearing in the distance, at the edge of the lake, pocked with the open foundations of missing buildings, the entire town pulled from its sockets and dragged somewhere beyond the mountains to the north.

Hear that, Mummy?

Behind the wind, there was another sound. Kathleen took George's good hand in hers and led him back onto the road. She heard a rumbling she could not place. She paused and tried to identify the sound. It was not thunder; it was not a train. Standing still she found that the sound was accompanied by a slight trembling of the earth. She began to walk again, toward the bend in the road. Just before she reached the bend, the din became less confused. She heard men shouting to one another and, in the unmistakable tones she had heard all of her life, at animals. There was a sound of harnesses and of beasts hauling at the yoke. And there was another sound—that of heavy timbers grating against one another.

There's something up there, Mum. George let go of Kathleen's hand and ran ahead. Kathleen called his name once, but he disappeared around the corner. The snow was heavy now, cascading out of the stone-colored sky in gouts. Kathleen rewrapped her scarf about her head and neck. She was cold; the tips of her toes stung and her nose dripped.

Kathleen turned the corner, eager for the first look at West Cove that any traveler had when she approached town from the south. The bend in the road was on the top of a hill and one looked down onto the town from above. Beyond the town was the lake, which stretched toward the horizon and during the winter was a vast white plain interrupted only by the humped black tufts of the four islands in its midst. Kathleen wondered whether the islands would be visible in the storm. She expected not. But instead of seeing the town and lake, she saw Dr. Box's house. It sat in the middle of the road, set on top of wooden trucks. The house and the trucks rested on a bed of massive logs, which had been lined up across a foundation of thick, planed beams set along the road. It was being dragged over the logs a foot at a time. Men wearing woolen red plaid coats and brimmed hats circled the house, carrying sledgehammers and crowbars, and yelled back and forth to one another around its corners. A flatbed truck idled behind the house. Its open bed was loaded with four enormous iron jacks. George stood in the road, halfway between the house and his mother. He turned from the house to her and she held a hand out toward him. She reached her son and took his hand and they walked up alongside the house, keeping to the side of the road, nearly in the ditch. The men ignored them or nodded their heads once distractedly in Kathleen's direction. Each time the house lurched forward, it proceeded along on the logs, which rolled beneath it over the beams. Kathleen saw at once that the process must be nearly impossibly slow; the house could be moved forward only six or eight feet at a time before the men would have to raise it up on the jacks and realign the logs beneath it and take up the timbers over which it just had been rolled and relay them in front of it.

As mother and son came abreast of the front corner of the house, they saw that it was being drawn by eight yoke of titanic oxen. The oxen were yoked in a train and harnessed to the house by chains as thick as Kathleen's wrists. A man marched up and down the length of the team with a bullwhip, cursing and whipping the beasts on their rumps. The oxen heaved and steamed in the cold. Each time the man yelled and cracked his whip, there was a rippling of wood and leather and iron as the chains fastened to the house snapped tight and each successive pair of oxen strained into the weight of the house and the building ground forward an inch or two, its windows rattling, its frame vibrating, and then the man with the whip yelled, Take yeere rest dogs, and the sixteen animals stopped pulling all at once, as if they were a circus act. The man was Ezra Morrell, George's best friend Ray Morrell's father.

Standing off to the side of the road, keeping slightly ahead of the progress of his home and business, was Dr. Box. He was dressed like the other men, except that his hat and his eyeglasses were of better quality. The eyeglasses were justified because of his profession; the town physician simply needed the best eyes he could get. The hat was his one public indulgence, the one symbol of his status in West Cove which he permitted himself. It came from a shop in London, where Dr. Box liked to say that there was an exact replica of his head in wood, around which each year a new hat was fitted for the real head thousands of miles away. (When he could not find his stethoscope or a tongue depressor, he'd say that the heads were mixed up—that the real head was in London and the wooden one in West Cove.) Otherwise, he wore the same wool coat of red plaid, the same dark wool pants, the same heavy boots, which laced up nearly to his knees. He munched on the stem of a pipe, now and then taking it from his mouth to say, That's it, boys! Or, Careful, fellas. Mother Box'll skin me if anything happens to the castle! When he saw Kathleen and George coming along, he made a show of stepping back, bowing slightly, and sweeping a hand across the space in front of himself for Kathleen to pass, and then snapped to attention and saluted George.

Come along, ma'am. Come along, sergeant. Just moving HQ closer to the line!

I'm sorry to interrupt, Doctor, Kathleen said, standing behind George with her hands resting on his shoulders. It's just that yesterday—

Dr. Box yanked his pipe from his mouth and set his large, slightly stained teeth together in a way to show that he was listening as a professional. Before Kathleen could continue, however, he saw George's bandaged hand.

Well, soldier, hurt in the line of duty, I see. Let's take a look.

Kathleen urged George forward a step and he shyly allowed the doctor to take his hand.

Don't worry, sergeant, I'll be careful. Dr. Box squatted and unwound the bandages. When he saw the puncture marks, he turned George's hand over and back twice, whistled, and said, A dog got you, huh, soldier? George looked at his mother.

Kathleen said, Well, it was an accident. We didn't—

I'm afraid you're going to need a stitch or two on the deepest cuts, the doctor said. Nothing broken, but you'll be sore for a good while. You'll probably feel it for longer, maybe even when you're an old man. Who's the dog? We need to see about rabies.

Kathleen said, That's the thing, Doctor. Can I— Could we— The doctor looked up from George's hand.

Yes, yes, of course, ma'am. Of course. He wound the bandages back around George's hand. Listen, sergeant, he said to George, your mother and I need to talk for a minute, so let's get you someplace warm. Dan! Danny! The doctor put his hand against George's back and steered him toward the idling truck. The driver's window was down and a man sat at the wheel, his head tilted outside the cab, smoking a cigarette. He looked up when the doctor called his name.

Danny, roll that window up and let this soldier

warm up in there; he's been injured in the line of duty!

The man, Dan Cooper, cinched his lips around the cigarette and pulled his head back into the truck cab. He rolled up the window, opened the truck door, and stepped down off the truck.

All yours, Doc, he said.

There you go. That's it, sergeant, the doctor said, helping George up into the passenger seat. You just mark time here and your mother and I'll be done in a jiff.

The cab of the truck warmed up quickly. The seat bench was covered in cracked brown leather. George felt broken seat springs through the bottom of his coat. Old manuals and newspapers and a coffee mug lined with the silt of long-since-evaporated coffee cluttered the space between him and the driver's seat. The glass steamed over and George watched the men and oxen and the moving house turn to phantoms in a silver mist. He remembered stories that his father had told him about ghost ships that had foundered on the rocks off the coast a hundred years ago but whose mournful, doomed crews and splintering keels could still be heard on foggy nights.

Kathleen and the doctor talked for ten minutes, toward the end of which George saw his mother bow her head and cover her face in her hands. He had never seen his mother cry and he knew it was about his father and that it was serious. Dr. Box hugged Kathleen to himself with one arm, patted her on the back twice, and then let go. He marched towards the truck. George looked past him to the blurry vision of his mother through the glass. She wiped her face on the sleeve of her coat and shook herself as if to slough off her weeping with the snow. She turned her face up toward the sky for a moment. Dr. Box grabbed the truck door open and saluted George.

Okay, sergeant, we're headed on ahead into town, where I can get you back into fighting shape.

George climbed down from the truck and went to his mother. Her face was flushed and her eyes red. She smiled at George and took his hand.

It's okay, Georgie, she said. George noticed for the first time that his mother was still a young woman. Dr. Box conferred with Dan Cooper, who had taken up his seat in the truck again, and two other men and then went back to Kathleen and George.

Ready, troops?

Kathleen said, It seems so sad—your house out in the middle of the road. She began to weep again.

Oh, poor Mrs. Crosby. There, there. We have to do something. It's time for us to do something. We're going to take care of everything.

Kathleen chopped wood, shaken. Howard was still on his rounds. The girls were in the parlor, doing needlepoint and keeping an eye on Joe, who was having a conversation with Ursula, a bearskin rug that he treated like one of the family pets. George slept upstairs, on top of Kathleen and Howard's bed. The wind was still up. But it will soften and die down when it gets dark, she thought. Wisps of snow were still on the wind, too, sweet and sharp. The sun was going down. It sank into the stand of beech trees beyond the back lot, lighting their tops, so that their bare arterial branches turned to a netting of black vessels around brains made of light. The trees lolled under the weight of those luminescent organs growing at the tops of their slender trunks. The brains murmured among themselves. They kept counsel and possessed a wintery wisdom—cold scarlet and opaline minds, brief and burnished, flaring in the metallic blue of dusk. And then they were gone. The light drained from the sky and the trees and funneled to a point on the western horizon, where it seemed to be swallowed by the earth. The branches of the trees were darknesses over the lesser dark of dusk. Kathleen thought, That is like Howard's brain—lit and used up and then dark. Lit too brightly. How much light does the mind need? Have use for? Like a room full of lamps. Like a brain full of light. She patted her coat pocket to feel the folded prospectus for the Eastern Maine State Hospital in Bangor, located *on top of Hepatica Hill overlooking the beautiful Penobscot River*. When Dr. Box had given her the brochure, her first thought had been to remember that the hospital had originally been called the Eastern Maine Insane Hospital. But the pictures in the brochure showed clean rooms and a broad, sunny campus and a huge brick building with four wings that looked to her like a grand hotel. The idea of a hotel seemed benevolent rather than cruel, seemed, in the suddenly alien backyard, full of glowing, leaky, vanishing brains, a warm, safe shelter that she envisioned as if she were a famished and half-frozen traveler on a planet made of ice, breaching a hill and catching sight of a lodge with lights in every window and smoke pouring from the chimneys and people gathered together, luxuriating in the dreamlike delight that comes from grateful strangers sharing sanctuary. The brochure was not in either of her coat pockets, and Kathleen realized that she must have placed it somewhere in her room when she helped George onto her bed.

George slept on top of his parents' bed. He lay curled up around his bitten hand. The bandages on the hand were tight, and in his shallow sleep a black dog held his hand in its mouth. The dog looked up into George's eyes and George knew that the dog would bite his hand if he tried to remove it. The dog would never move. It would never tire nor need to eat or sleep, and the thought that he would never be able to move again, but could only sit still, with his hand in the dog's mouth, for the rest of his life terrified George. He panicked and, by reflex, yanked his hand back. The dog's jaws sprang like a trap and the first pressure from the bite startled him awake. He whimpered for his mother. The room was cold and the blue in the windows so dim that it did not seem to be light, but the cold itself, which seemed to pry between the bed and his body, where the only warmth was. George shuddered and whimpered again and tried to burrow deeper into the bed, but he lay on top of the covers and could not get warm. Oh, Mummy, he groaned, and rose up onto an elbow. He looked at his bitten hand. The bandages seemed luminescent, as if the last light in the room might be coming from them. George felt his blood pulsing against them in his palm. The hand ached. He wanted to call for his mother again, but he heard the *tock-tock* of the hatchet in the yard. In the dark and the cold, it sounded as if his mother was chopping at rock, not wood, and a trace of his dream about the dog made him suddenly feel as if he would have to spend the rest of his life freezing and stranded on the bed with a crushed hand, listening to his mother uselessly chopping at stone out beyond the window fitted with panes of black ice, when what he most needed was to be curled up in her warm lap, with her warm hands on his face and her soft, quiet voice cooing to him that everything was all right. Instead, George sat upright and swung his legs over the side of the bed. He stood up and slid a foot forward in the total darkness of the floor, testing for the edge of the cable rug or a stray shoe that might trip him. He shuffled toward where the door was. He held his bitten hand limply above his head, as if he were crossing a river, and patted at the dark with his good hand until he felt the corner of his mother's bureau, which stood to the left of the door. He opened the door onto deeper darkness still. Rather than risking the hallway and the stairs, George tapped his fingers along the top of the bureau until he felt the lamp. He lifted the glass and set it down and felt for the box of matches. He held the matchbox against his stomach with the heel of his bitten hand and struck a match. The top of the bureau appeared and the image of him holding the match appeared in the lamp glass. There was a pamphlet next to the lamp, with a photograph of a building that looked to him like a school, called the Eastern Maine State Hospital. George realized that this was what Dr. Box had given to his mother after he had finished with the stitches in George's hand (there had only been four, and they had not hurt at first). Underneath the picture of the building, a caption read *Northern and Eastern Maine's care facility for the insane and feebleminded.* George touched the match to the lamp wick and light swelled up and out into the room. The light resolved the furniture and the walls and the floor and ceiling and George's eyes as if it were liquid. He opened the pamphlet and began to read. *Patients at the hospital experience relief from the frantic modern world, which aggravates so many cases of insanity. They enjoy sessions of hydrotherapy, extended periods of bedrest, harvesting crops, and tending the piggery. They also make and repair furniture and do the laundry. . . .*

Never you mind that, George. It's time to come down and get dinner. Kathleen had come upstairs without George noticing. George started when she spoke, and suddenly his head and his neck and his legs and his arms all ached and he felt feverish. Kathleen saw that he felt a kind of humiliation at being caught reading the pamphlet and at knowing just what it meant, even though it was something he should not even know about. She, too, suddenly suffered the weight of the day and felt cold and hungry and impatient.

My bureau is not yours to dig around, she said. She snatched the brochure from George's hands and shooed him out of her room and toward the stairs. Go get your brother ready to eat and tell your sisters to pour everyone a glass of milk. Go.

Yes, Mum. George stifled an urge to burst into tears. He went downstairs. Kathleen folded the brochure in half and stuffed it into a wool sock, which she tucked under a sweater at the back of her bottom bureau drawer.

That night, Kathleen and the children ate dinner without Howard, who was still not back from his rounds by seven o'clock. Afterward, she took up mending a pair of Joe's overalls in her rocking chair next to the woodstove. Darla and Margie played with two dolls, which they pretended were Susan B. Anthony and Betsy Ross preparing tea for George Washington and Andrew Jackson. Darla hopped Susan B. Anthony over to Betsy Ross, who was already sitting at the table, double-checking the tea service.

Darla made Susan B. Anthony bow to Betsy Ross and say, Happy New Year, Betsy!

Margie stood Besty Ross up and made her curtsy. And happy 1927 to you, Ms. Anthony!

Darla said, No, Margie, it's *1776*.

George sat on the couch, holding a book called *Mark the Match Boy* open on his lap with his injured hand and an apple in the other. He stared at the print but did not read. He thought about his father, who had bitten him and who was a madman about to be taken to the madhouse. It suddenly occurred to him that his brother, Joe, would be sent to the madhouse, too, sooner or later.

For years, an old bearskin rug of indeterminate origin had been lying in a far corner of the parlor. Sometimes, on cold nights, when the family gathered in the parlor, the children sat on it, pretending that they were riding a bear in a circus. Howard had named the rug Ursula. It was a ragged, mangy thing, with a bald patch running from its snout to between its eye sockets, which either had been pitted of their original glass eyes or simply left empty. The previous winter, George had inserted marbles in the sockets, one a milky green with gold sparkles, the other obsidian black. The black eye

made the bear look alive. The milky green eye made
her look as if she were half-blind, or as if she had one eye
on another world, since the gold sparkles in the green
looked like a tiny whirlpool of stars spinning inside a
cataract. George took a bite of his apple and watched
Joe, who jumped on the rug and pretended he was
riding the bear and then rolled off it as if it had
bucked him.

Stop that fussing around, Joe, Kathleen said.

Joe sprang up, smiling, and stepped toward George.
He pointed back to the rug and said, George, that
Ursula looks like she's fixing for to bite me!

George waited until Saturday to run away. He hitched
Prince Edward to his father's wagon and led the animal
and wagon out to the road, holding the reins tightly and
walking right next to the mule and whispering to it, urg-
ing it, shushing it. When he was out of sight of the
house, he mounted the wagon and snapped the reins
and said, Hya, boy, not in the manner of his father, who
merely flicked the leather leads and made a clicking
sound with his tongue against his back teeth, but of his
friend Ray Morrell's father, who talked with a strange
accent George had never heard before and would never
hear again, and who seemed to have stepped out of
some bank of mist on the other side of which was, perfectly preserved—or, not even preserved, but still actual
—the previous century. Ray's father Ezra, owned sixteen

oxen. When he drove them, he said, Hya, hya, boys or, Work it, ye dogs. Mr. Morrell was the only person George ever knew who used the word *ye*.

So George said, Hya, boy, and Prince Edward barely noticed and started to walk at a pace a little slower than usual, as if registering his awareness that this was not his usual route, not his usual driver, not his usual cue. The sunny weekend morning, the lackadaisical mule, and the extra heaviness of the slow rate imparted by the bulk of the wagon conspired to dilute George's half notions of speed and flight and pursuit and evasion. In his mind, he, during school the previous days, had seen trees flying by, alternating trunks and light flicking by. He saw hounds baying and scrambling past a thicket of reeds and cat-o'-nine-tails at the edge of water and, after they had passed, the stalks parting and his own head rising half out of the water, alert, sharp, animallike. Now, he inched along in full daylight atop a wagon as big as a house and as noisy as a suitcase full of Turkish cymbals. For the first time, he wondered about what all of those drawers were packed with. He realized that he had formed a vague conception of the wagon's inventory—brushes, mops, pots, pipes, socks, suspenders, polish—a single picture that appeared in his mind whenever he thought about the wagon. It came up like a road sign, a billboard, or an advertisement—simple and all-encompassing and, he now understood, cursory and distorted. He peered over the side of the wagon. I couldn't even say what wood the drawers are made from, he thought.

When the turnoff to his friend Ray Morrell's farm came up, George took it without thinking. He was nearly at the old curing house, now a toolshed, or at least shed for odd planks and hoops and handles and blades of wood and iron for which there was no longer use, each artifact having split or worn out or dulled to the very end of usefulness, so that not even Ray's father, the most frugal farmer in a countryside of frugal and impoverished farmers, could nail it, tie it, or hammer it back into place and eke out one more execution of whatever task the piece of wood or metal was supposed to perform. The curing house was at the end of another turnoff along the dirt tracks that led from the main road (which was dirt as well, this far out of town, but of well-packed and -tended dirt) to the Morrells'. George had taken both turns without thinking. The curing shed was where he and Ray Morrell went and smoked and played cribbage and told stories and jokes after they had finished working for Ray's father—milking the cow or sweeping the yard or, most often, unyoking and feeding and inspecting Ray's father's giant oxen.

(Ray Morrell already, at twelve years old, had the air of a chaste, fastidious old bachelor, someone who knew about commemorative coins and prevailing winds and who, already, had a taste for the turpentinelike bathtub gin his father always had a bottle of stashed away under the basement stairs. And many years after he had enough money to comfortably buy better, Ray continued to buy the most wretched gin he could find, until his swollen liver gave out. He was pleased to allow people to think that his taste for rotgut was because of thrift born of his childhood dirt-farmer poverty, when, in fact, it was because he was forever soothed by the memories of drinking hooch that could have doubled as paint thinner in the old curing house with dusty blades of sunlight stabbing through the gaps in its wall boards during afternoons after school with his best friend in the world, George Washington Crosby.)

Ezra was known throughout the county and beyond as the man to call when you needed something big pulled. This was the source of many crude jokes. The smallest of his oxen stood at just under six feet at the shoulders; the tallest, over seven and a half. The oxen were one of his two passions. The other was baseball, which he followed in the papers every week, nearly committing all of the box scores to memory, so that as he plowed his fields or whipped his team (which he hired out in pairs, from two to the full regiment of sixteen, and which he himself always oversaw), he muttered batting averages and runs batted in and earned- run averages out loud to himself, which, overheard, were simply random-sounding streams of numbers. The statistic that gave Ezra Morrell the most pleasure to contemplate was that of the players' batting averages, and every time he acquired a new ox, he named it after the most recent batting champion from the American League. When he cracked the whip, then, he could be heard variously harassing Ed Delehanty, Elmer Flick, George Stone, Tris Speaker, George Sisler, Harry Heilman, Babe Ruth, one of the three Napoleon Lajoies, or six Ty Cobbs (because he had more oxen than different batting champs, so that when he ran out, he started back at the beginning and named the animals for the different years the same players had won). Hya, Napoleon One, ye dog, lean into it, Ezra would yell. That's no four-twenty-two effort! Unlike other fans of the sport, Ezra took no pleasure in talking about the game with anyone else. When his son dared ask how the great Cobb had fared on the last road trip, Ezra cuffed the boy on the ear, and said, The great Cobb Three has shat his stall full again, ye chatty pup. Now go clean it up before ye're behind with the feed.

George tied Prince Edward to a tree in front of the shed. The inside of the shed felt colder than the outside. Sunlight streamed through cracks between the log cribbing of the walls and seams between boards in the roof where outside the shingles had come loose and blown away. The light flowing in from the roof dropped toward the floor in rectangular planes, which were broken by the heavy rafters. Some of the rafters still had curing hooks hanging from them. There was an abandoned barn swallow's nest in the crook of one of the rafters and a support beam. A dusty hill of droppings remained on the floor beneath the nest.

George stood in the shed. He was suddenly aware that if he was running away, this was not the place to go. To run away meant away. He had never been away. Away was the French Revolution or Fort Sumter or the Roman Empire. Maybe, Boston, three hundred miles south. He had no idea what was in the three hundred miles between here and Boston.

George poked through the pile of ashes and cigarette stubs next to the three nail kegs he and Ray had set up so that each could sit and the cribbage board that George had taken from home could be set between them. He found a butt with two or three drags left to it. He pinched it by the very end. There were no matches. He pitched the cigarette back onto the pile.

A door lay lengthwise against the far wall of the shed. It was from the old Budden place, long since burned down. It was mammoth: made of oak two inches thick. Its hinges and handle had been hacked at. The side facing out into the shed was charred and striated by fire. When George and Ray sat in the shed smoking whatever they had been able to find, which was rolled corn husks as often as it was tobacco, and playing cribbage with the board George had stolen from his own house, they liked to recite the story about the winter of '06, when the snow was twelve feet high and the sun didn't shine for three months and Budden went mad

and took the big ax into the house and staved all of the
furniture and piled all the broken pieces together in the
middle of the parlor and doused it all with kerosene and
took a match to it. The hack marks in the door were not
from Budden. They were from the volunteer firemen
and neighbors (who were the same thing: each a neighbor, each a volunteer firefighter, because you were a
fireman if you were a man fighting a fire) who had tried
to chop their way through the door to get to Mrs.
Budden and the children. By the time they realized that
the door was too thick and that they should try to go
through a window or the back door, the fire was too
ferocious to be able to do anything but leap off the
porch. Then, just as they realized this, just as they col-
lectively understood that the door could not be
breached, something inside the house exploded and the
door wrenched from its hinges and blew outward, plowing the men in front of it, so that they and it landed in
the front walkway, they on the ground, it on them—the
side which now faced out into the shed burning and
gushing smoke. But here was the thing, the reason for
the recitation and repetition of the story: When the fire
was finally put out, and they found the bodies, Tom
Budden's corpse in the kitchen but also one adult (a
woman, it was determined) and two children, spooned
up against one another within the boundaries of the
iron frame of the Budden's big double bed (the mattress,
the sheets, the blankets burned away), calm and peace-

ful as if they were taking an afternoon nap, cooked to
smoldering crisps, and whom everybody assumed were
Mrs. Budden and the Budden children, and so the town
started to make funeral preparations, Mr. Potter meas-
uring the charred corpses as best he could to make the
coffins, Mrs. Budden and the children showed up from
Worcester, where they had been visiting her mother.
No one had ever figured out who that woman and those
children were who had been sleeping in the Budden
house on the afternoon Tom Budden went berserk and
set it all on fire.

George crawled behind the door and lay down. He
put his bitten hand against the cold wood and imagined
it as scorching hot, imagined it holding back a tremen-
dous fire, which battered and seared it and built up
behind it and blew it loose from its hinges. The fire
thumped on the other side of the door. George lowered
his hand to his lap. He tried to squeeze it into a fist. It
was still too sore to fully close. Once again, he fell first
to wishing that his father would just disappear from the
face of the earth—not die, not be put away, but just
miraculously suddenly not be—and then to wishing that
his father were a child himself and that he be bitten by
his own father, so he could suffer how awful it was to
have been attacked by his own sire. George's feelings
had moved back and forth between these two thoughts
the entire week, except for when he had actually seen
his father, who had for the most part stayed away from

the house the rest of that week, and had kept to corners and alongside walls and just beyond doorways, like a kicked dog, when he had been home. Whenever George saw his father in the house, he had to keep from crying at being so angry for having a mad father whom he loved and pitied and hated. He tucked his injured hand into his coat and fell asleep. His breath steamed from his half-opened mouth in little clouds, which rolled upward, fragile, and broke apart against the underside of the door.

Kathleen said to Howard, George has run away.

He said, How do you know?

She said, He left Joe alone in the toolshed. He didn't split the wood. He didn't get the water. He didn't help Darla with her numbers. He took Prince Edward and your wagon.

He said, I don't think he'll get too far. He thought, I hope he makes it.

She said, What, exactly, are you going to sell today without your wagon?

He said, Kathleen.

She said, You can borrow Lady Godiva from the Levansellers. He can't be more than two miles away.

He said, Kathleen. But she was already walking back around the house to the tin washtub full of steaming soapy water and clothes.

*   *   *

Seems George's run away.

That so.

Yes, it is.

Well, I never.

Nor I.

The two men looked at the sky and then at the dirt yard ringed in dirty snow where chickens strutted and pecked. Jack Levanseller pursed his lips and blew air from his mouth.

Howard looked toward the Levanseller barn, which was more like a large garage fitted out to stable the old nag Jack Levanseller had bought for his daughter, Emily, when she just had to have a horse and had cried and said things at meals like, I don't *want* potatoes; I want a *horse*! for a week, until her father finally could not take the twelve-year-old's theatrics anymore and had gone to the horse farm over in Dexter and bought the cheapest, most run down, wheezy creature on the lot for six dollars. When she saw the horse, with its runny nose and scabby ears and its ribs as visible as the staves of a barrel and its pelvis, too, she screamed, What is *that*! and her father had said, That is your horse and it looks hungry. And cold, too. And it was true; even though it was the end of June and nearly eighty degrees, the horse seemed to be shivering. Jack slapped the horse on its bony rump and, noticing that the beast was missing a good amount of its hair, and that it was a mare, said, This is your horse and her name is Lady Godiva. Now go get a pail of water and some hay and that old blue blanket and start taking care of your new horse. Emily cried, I don't want that disgusting creature! I'll bet you can't even *ride* it! And she had refused to have anything to do with the wretched beast, so that her father had taken care of it from the moment he brought it onto his property and complained to anyone who would listen about how he lost a lot more than six dollars on that horse, considering how much of his time and oats he spent keeping the thing till it decided to die.

Howard said, Lady Godiva—

Jack said, She's a dollar a day.

Howard said, A dollar.

Jack said, Plus oats.

Plus oats.

The men looked at their hands, at the chickens.

Well, I suppose I can walk.

I suppose.

Well, thanks, Jack.

Don't mention it, Howard.

Howard walked past his house without telling Kathleen that Levanseller wanted a dollar for Lady Godiva and that he had decided to walk. She would make him go back, even though a dollar was twice what he made most days, after he paid Cullen back the cost of its brushes and hairpins and the penny or two profit afterward. He walked past the house, with its tall front windows and chipping gray paint and rotting unpainted shutters, sitting in its nest of winter grass and snow. It was bright outside and dark inside, but as he passed he shaded his eyes and looked into the dining room and could just see the table and empty chairs.

After Howard has passed beyond sight of the house, Kathleen stops her washing, dries her hands on the front of her apron, and goes into the house. She climbs the stairs to her bedroom on tiptoe, even though she does not have to hide the fact that she is going to her room. She enters her room and opens the bottom drawer of her bureau. The bureau stands directly next to the doorway. She fishes around in the back of the drawer and pulls out the wool sock in which she hid the brochure for the mental hospital. She removes the brochure from the sock and without looking at it places it in full view on the corner of the top of the bureau and returns to her washing.

It was not difficult for Howard to find his son. The fresh wagon and mule tracks left from the yard, away from town. Howard walked along the road and looked at the winter weeds poking up from the new snow. There was more variety than Howard had ever noticed. There were papery shells of burst pods and thorns and whitish nubs at the ends of pannicles. Some were bent over, broken-backed, with their tops buried in the snow,

as if they had been smothered in the frost. The inter-
locking network of stalks and branches and creepers was
skeletal, the fossil yard of an extinct species of fine-
boned insectoid creatures. All of these bones, then, seemed
to have been stained by sun and earth from an original
living white to brown, and not the tough fibrous flower
and seed-spilling green they actually once had been.
Howard wondered about a man who had never seen
summer, a winter man, examining the weeds and making this inference—that he was looking at an ossuary.
The man would take that as true and base his ideas of
the world on that mistake. He would concoct narratives
about when those thorny animals picked through the
brush and fields, sketch outlandish guesses, publish
papers, give talks in opulent rooms to serious men all
wearing the same formal suits, draw conclusions, get it
all wrong. Howard thought, I do not even know if that
is ragweed or Queen Anne's lace.

When he came to the turnoff for Ezra Morrell's
farm, he saw the wagon tracks turn with it. There was
a moment of sorrow, disappointment, and deep love
for his son, whom he at that second wished had had a
chance of real escape. Never mind why or whether or
who or what consequence or ramification—the wake
of sorrow and bitterness and resentment you would
trail behind you, probably mostly for me—I just wish
that you had made it beyond the bounds of this cold
little radius, that when the archaeologists brush off

this layer of our world in a million years and string off the boundaries of our rooms and tag and number every plate and table leg and shinbone, you would not be there; yours would not be the remains they would find and label *juvenile male*; you would be a secret, the existence of which they would never even be aware to try to solve. An image arose in Howard's mind of an archaeologist examining the small bones of George's hand and explaining to his colleagues that the boy whose bones these had been had at one time been bitten by another person, an adult, perhaps as part of some savage ritual or because people were more like wild animals in this place in those times than had ever previously been imagined.

Howard stepped into the shed. Light came between the log cribbing where first the original grass and mud and then the wadded-up comics pages from Sunday newspapers had dissolved.

George. Where are you?

Here I am, Daddy.

Where?

Here. George crawled out from behind the old door.

Howard's eyes adjusted to the dim interior of the shed. He made out George's face peeping from behind the old door. He remembered the fire. He remembered the story about the woman and the children. He thought, My son hiding behind the ruins, my son hiding behind the last burned token of a house. Houses

can be ghosts, too, just like people. And when he
thought this, it was because he realized that whenever
he imagined (Am haunted by, really, he thought, because
that is what ghosts are, what they do, whether they
knock plates of off shelves or blow a door open at
night or simply present themselves in our minds, it is
all haunting) that woman and her children, they were
always in the house, which, like them, was gone from
this earth. And we were like the men giving papers on
the skeletons lining the ditch; we were certain the
bones were those of Addie Budden and the kids, but
they were not. So there is my son, hiding behind the
last vestige of a house transformed from timber into
ash into the dimming memories of those who still
remember it. If the door survives us all, it will be, like
most things, just another relic sitting (somewhere,
somewhere not here, even, but somewhere unlikely—
in the grass of the plains, a swamp island in the bayou,
down an Arctic crevasse among other artifacts perhaps
not yet even made but heading towards made, being
pulled toward being made (or fashioned: made in the
sense that they are and always have been latent in living wood, in underground seams, in stars and the
black sky), but even then, before made, rushing toward
their being unmade and perhaps made again. Everything is made to perish; the wonder of anything at all
is that it has not already done so. No, he thought. The
wonder of anything is that it was made in the first

place. What persists beyond this cataclysm of making and unmaking?

So there is my son, already fading. The thought frightened him. The thought frightened because as soon as it came to him, he knew that it was true. He understood suddenly that even though his son knelt in front of him, familiar, mundane, he was already fading away, receding. His son was fading away before his eyes and that fact was inevitable, even though Howard understood, too, that the fading was yet to begin in any actual sense, that at that moment he and his son, the father standing in the dimness, the son kneeling and partly obscured by the charred door, were still only heading, not yet arrived, toward the point where the fading would begin. Howard simply knew that that point was coming and that he somehow had caught a glimpse of its existence beforehand, as if the moment were like the burned door: an object sitting in the shed, leaning among the rusty old saws and spades and rakes, but also as unimaginable and unknowable as his extinct creatures with grass bones.

Mother's worried, George. You have to come back.

I know, Dad.

George stood and walked to his father. Howard put his hand on his son's shoulder for a moment and looked into the boy's eyes. He seemed about to speak but then smiled and removed his hand. George climbed onto the cart and Howard untied Prince Edward. The mule responded much more readily to Howard's guidance, and father and son drove back to their house without speaking.

The next evening, Howard passed by his house before he realized he had seen a brochure for a place called the Eastern Maine State Hospital that morning on his wife's dresser and that she was planning to have him committed there. He passed out of the center of town, heading south. Dinner was on the table in the house. Everyone sat at their seats, wordless, waiting for him to turn in to the dirt driveway and tether Prince Edward and give him hay and then to come inside and say grace, which he always ended with the words, And God let us perceive that there is nothing better than that a man should rejoice in his own work. Amen.

He had spoken no words to himself. No conscious thought precipitated his action, as if spending the whole day contemplating what he was going to do, had already done by the time he fitted words to the actions, which was to ride past the kitchen window that framed his family and leafed them in its gold light, would have diluted his resolve, would have led him to turn himself over to a fate that, had he thought about it, he would have accepted rather than acknowledge its implications. He could not have let himself be witness to the simultaneity of his wife passing him a plate of chicken or a basket of hot bread as she worked out her plans to have him taken away. Howard had assumed that their silence over his fits, over everything, stood for his gratefulness to her and her loyalty to him. He had assumed their silence was one of kindness offered and accepted.

The distance between Howard and his house lengthened and, as it did, segregated him from his life as if it were time. The smell of the wood oil and kerosene from the wagon made him think of the rooms and stairways he already knew he would never enter again and he realized that what he sat upon, the swaying cart full of products for cleaning, scrubbing, patching, organizing, maintaining domestic life, was a house. I am perched on a house, he thought. He thought, God let us perceive that there is nothing better than that a man should rejoice in his own work. God hear me weep because I let myself think all is well if I am fully stocked with both colors of shoe shine and beeswax for the wooden tables, sea sponge and steel wool for dirty dishes. God hear me weep as I fill out receipts for tin buckets, and slip hooch into coat pockets for cash, and tell people about my whip-smart sons and beautiful daughters. God know my shame as I push my mule to exhaustion, even after the moon and Venus have risen to preside over the owls and mice, because I am not going back to my family—my wife, my children—because my wife's silence is not the forbearance of decent, stern people who fear You; it is the quiet of outrage, of bitterness. It is the quiet of biding time. God forgive me. I am leaving.

There was an early January thaw and it had been raining all day, but just before sunset the storm clouds passed and it rained only in the trees. Steam lifted off of the snow. Trees stood half in light, half in shadow as the sun lowered and striped the world in a weave half of itself, half of the approaching evening. Howard drove Prince Edward late into the night. The mule was difficult to handle. It tried to turn around several times. Several times the mule stopped and refused to go forward. Finally, Howard gave in and stopped for the night twenty miles south of his now-former home. He turned off the road at a clearing where for some reason the snow had melted away and there was a circle of grass wide enough on which to park the cart. He unhitched Prince Edward and fed him and then fed himself by eating the lunch he had saved that afternoon because, even though he had not permitted himself to think consciously about his flight, some part of him had known to save the ham sandwich and cold potatoes for later.

Howard leaned against one of the wagon's rear wheels and stared at the candled sky and looked back at the candle he had lit and wished it would turn blue with the light of the stars and that the stars would turn gold like burning wicks. He wondered if Kathleen and the children were still sitting at the dining room table in front of their cold food.

So what if he could give them circus ponies and silk dresses? What, too, of cinders and hair shirts and bites

on their hands and feet? Howard imagined that neither would bring peace to his wife's heart. Her piety
depended too much on a pose of forbearance, a face of
oppression. Red ribbons served as well as stove ash.
That she made a point to eat only the gristliest chicken
bits, the burned biscuits, the mealiest potatoes, while
she complained that his children were, variously, weak-
minded, hysterical, or sickly, and seemed to imply that
such afflictions were the result of the lack of a good
piece of steak or a new bonnet, was only circumstance;
were she installed on a throne at a twelve-course ban-
quet table teaming with all of God's creatures brought
from both air and field, trussed and roasted and swimming in their own succulent juices, she would heap her
plate with the most exquisite victuals and lament that
his feeble offspring were the way they were because
they had it too well and what they really needed was a
vat of cold porridge and a tureen full of dirt.

Howard thought, Is it not true: A move of the head,
a step to the left or right, and we change from wise,
decent, loyal people to conceited fools? Light changes,
our eyes blink and see the world from the slightest dif-
ference of perspective and our place in it has changed
infinitely: Sun catches cheap plate flaking—I am a tinker; the moon is an egg glowing in its nest of leafless
trees—I am a poet; a brochure for an asylum is on the
dresser—I am an epileptic, insane; the house is behind
me—I am a fugitive. His despair had not come from the

fact that he was a fool; he knew he was a fool. His despair came from the fact that his wife saw him as a fool, as a useless tinker, a copier of bad verse from two-penny religious magazines, an epileptic, and could find no reason to turn her head and see him as something better.

He slept in the grass beneath the cart. The moon rose and arced above his sleeping form. Night played its play while he dreamed of empty rooms and abandoned hallways. A small pack of wolves came from the hills. They circled his cart once, sniffed, and padded away. He woke once just before dawn and thought he saw lights in the trees, but a slight wind rose through the grass up and into the branches and scattered them away, so he closed his eyes again.

He woke to Prince Edward snuffling at the grass near his head. He grabbed for his hat because the mule had eaten it off his head once before, leaving the beast ill and gassy and he behind it with teary eyes and a sunburned nose. Birds traded their chirps and whistles of alarm and warning. It was early enough so that the grass in which he lay beneath the cart was still blue and gray and purple. Outside the shadow of the cart, the snow was blue. The rainwater on the trees had frozen overnight and turned into sheaths of ice that refracted the gold light from the rising sun into silver light that glittered in the breeze. A crop of mushrooms had somehow grown overnight in the grass next to Howard beneath the cart. He examined them and was slightly alarmed at how large they had grown from nothing in such a short time and in such cold.

3

It had never occurred to Howard to tell George about his own father. Howard thought to himself, That's right; my own father was always in the room upstairs at the walnut desk tucked under the eaves, composing. He was even there when we ate dinner and when I did my lessons. He would comment on this sometimes; he would say, What an odd thing, how I am here eating peas and there, too, scratching at my sermon. We said nothing, but a shiver would run through me at the thought of rising from the table at my father's left-hand side and passing into the narrow unadorned hallway and up the narrow stairs, which were the only way to the second floor, to the study, where I would see my father bent over his work. Sometimes I spent entire dinners imagining myself in a sort of loop where I continually went between my father at his desk and my father at the dinner table, always baffled in my intentions by his ability to be in two places at once and my limitation to only one. My father was a strange, gentle man.

A wind would come up through the trees, sounding like a chorus, so like a breath then, so sounding like a breath, the breath of thousands of souls gathering itself up somewhere in the timber lining the bowls and depressions behind the worn mountains the way thunderstorms did and crawling up their backs the way the thunderstorms did, too, which you couldn't hear, quite, but felt barometrically—a contraction or flattening as of tone as everything compressed in front of it, again, which you couldn't see, quite, but instead could almost see the result of—water flattening, so the light coming off of it shifted angles, the grass stiffening, so it went from green to silver, the swallows flitting over the pond all being pushed forward and then falling back to their original positions as they corrected for the change, as if the wind were sending something in front of it. The hair on my neck prickled from nape to crown, as if a current were passing through it, and as the current leapt off of the top of my head and if I had my back to the trees, I would feel the actual wind start up the back of my neck and ruffle my hair and the water and the grass and spin the swallows in its choral voice stirring all of the old unnamable sorrows in our throats, where our voices caught and failed on the scales of the old forgotten songs. My father would say, The forgotten songs we never really knew, only think we

remember knowing, when what we really do is understand at the same time how we have never really known
them at all and how glorious they must really be. My
father would tell me this from his desk up under the eaves
while I was across the pond tracking otters or fishing off
the fallen fir tree near the point. I would hear his voice
and look across the water to the white of our house, just
visible behind the line of trees, to where I knew his open
window was inhaling and exhaling the plain white curtains my mother had insisted on in the name of minimal
domestic propriety. He whispered in my ears: Bring string
and bottle caps and broken glass; bring candy wrappers
and nickels and smooth stones; bring fallen feathers and
fingernail parings; the old songs have shaken our small
home to the ground again and we must rebuild. And our
house across the pond would flicker and then blink out,
disappear, because it had been such a fragile idea in the
first place. Then I would again be on the far shore, looking at where we would build our home, once we cleared
the woods and dug the foundation.

How can I not wonder what it would be like to sit in
that cold silver water, that cold stone water up to my
chin, the tangled marsh grass at the level of my eyes, sit
in the still water, in the still air, bright day behind me
lighting the face of everything under the dark millstone
cloud lid in front of me, watching the storm coming
from the north? There is my father whispering in my

ear, Be still, still, still. And yet you change everything. What was the marsh like, waiting for the storm before you came and kneeled in the water? It was like nothing. Watch after you leave the water, now cold and regretful, miles from home, certain of the belt on your backside, the cold shoulder, the extra chores; watch. Watch the water heal itself of your presence—not to repair injury but to offer itself again should you care to risk another strapping, because instead of the sky being dark and the trees and stones bright, the next time the sky will be bright but the world gloomy. Or there will be rain with no wind. Or wind and sun. Or a starry sky laced with clouds that look like cotton thread. You could not do better if you passed a thousand acts of Congress.

O, Senator, drop your trousers! Loosen your cravat! Eschew your spats and step into that shallow, teeming world of mayflies and dragonflies and frogs' eyes staring eye-to-eye with your own, and the silty bottom. Cease your filibuster against the world God gave you. Enough of your clamor, your embarrassing tendencies, your crooking of paths in the name of straightness. Enough of your calling ruin upon the Moor and the Hindoo, the Zulu and the Hun. None of it gains you a jot. Behold, and be a genius! At a breath, I shall disperse your world, your monuments of metal, your monuments of stone, and your brightly striped rags. They will scatter like so many pins and skittles. I shall

tire myself more quenching a candle in its sconce.
Phew! There: you are gone.

I should say that the sermons my father gave on Sundays
were bland and vague. Parishioners regularly drifted off
to sleep sitting up in their pews and it was common to
hear snoring coming from this or that corner of the
room. My father's voice droned on about the impor-
tance of every little creature in the field, enumerating
practically every crawling, swimming, flying beast he
could and reiterating that it, too, was as important as
any other of God's creations. And consider the rats in
the grain, he would say. And the barking crows, and the
squirrels collecting nuts. Are they, too, not God's creatures? And the foraging raccoon.

There was no correspondence between these inept
speeches with the passionate, even obsessive writing he
did up beneath the pitched roof. It seemed, in fact, that
the more time my father spent in his study composing, the
worse his sermons became, until they were practically no
more than incoherent mumbling, in the midst of which,
here and there, if one was actually listening, you could
pick out the name of the odd prophet or the citation of a
psalm or chapter or verse. The people of the town had little patience for mumbling, and what they at first must
have taken as perhaps an especially indirect intelligence,
one perhaps even given to constructing his sermons as
parables in emulation of Christ, they soon got fed up with

and began to complain about—first in discreet letters, then directly to my father on the way out of church. My father responded to this criticism with genuine surprise, as if shocked that what must have really been on his mind had not been included in his sermon. My goodness, Mrs. Greenleaf, he would say, I am so sorry the sermon was not to your liking. The path is narrow. I must have wavered, he would say, and look confused. This was the first sign that he had in some way become unhitched from our world and was already beginning to drift away.

Finally, the situation became so alarming to the congregation (after a particularly baffling Sunday-morning service, during which my father at one point clearly mentioned something about the devil being finally not so bad after all) that the parishioners demanded a special meeting to address their new minister's deteriorating condition. On the Wednesday morning he was to meet with the deacons and the congregation, my mother practically had to dress him herself. He was pale and unshaven and seemed like a child. My mother saw him and cried, What are you doing? We have to go to the church for your meeting. Good Lord, good Lord. Throughout my father's deterioration, my mother had kept her thoughts to herself. She cooked and ironed and kept his house and must have trusted at first that my father was in some sort of a slump, that his weak sermons and increased time working on them must be part of a natural ebb and flow in any minister's career.

Perhaps she even believed that he was going through a kind of healthy crisis of belief, one from which her husband would emerge with his faith refreshed and his convictions stronger than ever. Whatever she thought, she never spoke a word about it.

When my mother finally succeeded in getting my father shaved and into his clothes and off to the church, she ordered me to stay home from school and tend the house and be home when they returned. After they left, I sat at the kitchen table with my history book open to the chapter I was studying on Napoléon. There was a painting of him on a white horse and one of him leading a charge with his sword drawn and pointed toward an unseen enemy. I could not concentrate on the text. I worried about my father. Throughout his illness (that is the word that now, for the first time, came to my mind, and it shocked me and suddenly made me frightened), he had remained kind and remote toward me, as he had always been, but I had lately noticed him looking at me with a sort of wistfulness, as if he were not looking at me, but at a drawing or photograph of me, as if he were remembering me.

It seemed to me as if my father simply faded away. He became more and more difficult to see. One day, I thought he was sitting in his chair at his desk, writing. To all appearances, he scribbled at a sheet of paper. When I asked him where the bag for apple picking was, he disappeared. I could not tell whether he had been there in the first place or if I had asked my question to some lingering afterimage.

He leaked out of the world gradually, though. At first, he seemed merely vague or peripheral. But then he could no longer furnish the proper frame for his clothes. He would ask me a question from behind the box on which I sat shelling peas or peeling potatoes for my mother, and when I answered and received no reply back, I would turn around, to find his hat or belt or a single shoe sitting in the door frame as if placed there by a mischievous child. The end came when we could no longer even see him, but felt him in brief disturbances of shadows or light, or as a slight pressure, as if the space one occupied suddenly had had something more packed into it, or we'd catch some faint scent out of season, such as the snow melting into the wool of his winter coat, but on a blistering August noon, as if the last few times I felt him as another being rather than as a recollection, he had thought to check up on this world at the wrong moment and accidentally stepped from whatever wintry place he was straight into the dog days. And it seems that doing so only confirmed to him his fate to fade away, his being in the wrong place, so that during these startled visits, although I could not see him, I could feel his surprise, his bafflement, the dismay felt in a dream when you suddenly meet the brother you forgot you had or remember the infant you left on the hillside miles away, hours ago, because somehow you were distracted and somehow you came to believe in a different life and your shock at these terrible recollections, these sudden reunions, comes as much from your sorrow at what you have neglected as it does from dismay at how thoroughly and quickly you came to believe in something else. And that other world that you first dreamed is always better if not real, because in it you have not jilted your lover, forsaken your child, turned your back on your brother. The world fell away from my father the way he fell away from us. We became his dream.

Another time, I found him fumbling for an apple in the barrel we kept in the basement. I could just make him out in the gloom. Each time he tried to grab a piece of fruit, it eluded him, or I might say he eluded it, as his grasp was no stronger than a draft of air threading through a crack in a window. He succeeded once, after appearing to concentrate for a moment, in upsetting an apple from its place at the top of the pile, but it merely tumbled down along the backs of the other apples and came to rest against the mouth of the barrel. It seemed to me that even if I could pick an apple up with my failing hands, how could I bite it with my dissipating teeth, digest it with my ethereal gut? I realized that this thought was not my own but, rather, my father's, that even his ideas were leaking out of his former self. Hands, teeth, gut, thoughts even, were all simply more or less convenient to human circumstance, and as my father was receding from human circumstance, so, too, were all of these particulars, back to some unknowable froth where they might be reassigned to be stars or belt buckles, lunar dust or railroad spikes. Perhaps they already

were all of these things and my father's fading was
because he realized this: My goodness, I am made from
planets and wood, diamonds and orange peels, now and
then, here and there; the iron in my blood was once the
blade of a Roman plow; peel back my scalp and you will
see my cranium covered in the scrimshaw carved by an
ancient sailor who never suspected that he was whittling
at my skull—no, my blood is a Roman plow, my bones
are being etched by men with names that mean sea
wrestler and ocean rider and the pictures they are making are pictures of northern stars at different seasons,
and the man keeping my blood straight as it splits the
soil is named Lucian and he will plant wheat, and I cannot concentrate on this apple, this apple, and the only
thing common to all of this is that I feel sorrow so deep,
it must be love, and they are upset because while they
are carving and plowing they are troubled by visions of
trying to pick apples from barrels. I looked away and ran
back upstairs, skipping the ones that creaked, so that I
would not embarrass my father, who had not quite yet
turned back from clay into light.

Suppose that my mother helped my father dress on an
early April morning. It was dark and windy outside, with
flurries of snow swirling down from the sky as if they
were chips dropping from chiseled clouds, and the three
of us had been indoors together for four days as it rained
and blew and the rivers and lakes swelled and spread

beyond their banks. Two nights before, we had even seen Old Sabbatis paddling a canoe through the woods behind our house. My father was stooped and could not get his arms through his jacket by himself. And when my mother helped him, the sleeves of his jacket gathered those of his shirt and both rode up to his elbows as he pulled them too far up his arms. His head shook, and in his and my mother's struggles with his coat, his wide-brimmed hat was pushed to an odd angle, so that it looked as if my mother were straining to dress a scarecrow. My mother said to him in a voice that was both vexed and solicitous, Oh, Father, you know you're not supposed to put your hat on until the end. He seemed parched and worked his tongue in his mouth as if he were searching for water.

Suppose that my mother dressed my father in the parlor rather than their bedroom and that this frightened me, seeing, for example, my father's thin, pale legs naked in the room where he consoled widows. The shades in the two windows were drawn and my mother had not lit a lamp, so that they struggled in the thin light entering the room around the borders of the shades. I stood in the doorway to the kitchen, watching them. My father suffered a great indignity and I was helpless to restore him. That he and my mother should wrestle him into his clothes in the dark seemed furtive and awful. And yet, the thought of walking across the room and opening the shades and letting the raw, weak light pour down on them seemed worse, as if the least my father could be granted was that he be allowed to fall apart in the dark.

When he was dressed, my mother pointed my father to the kitchen. They walked together side by side in a sort of half embrace, my mother rubbing his back with one hand and holding one of his hands in the other, guiding him and soothing him, murmuring softly to him, watching his feet to make sure he did not trip over himself. I backed into the kitchen, and when they came through the door, my mother saw me and said, You'll have to make your own breakfast today, Howard, I'm taking Father. My father looked at me and nodded, the way you might when you first meet the acquaintance of a friend on the street. My mother opened the outside door and the light came in and carved every object in the kitchen into an ancient relic. I could not imagine what people had ever done with iron skillets or rolling pins. Through the door, beyond our yard, at the edge of the road, four men stood, all in black coats and black hats, waiting for my mother and my father. They were my father's friends, men from the church. I stood in the doorway and watched my mother and father reach the men, who gathered around them and escorted them to a coach drawn by four horses, which waited for them at a respectable distance and which was driven by a man I did not recognize, who sat hunkered into his coat and scarf to keep out the wind and the snow and the rain, which had begun again. The men helped my father into the coach first and then my mother, a reversal of their usual and rit-ually observed manners, which seemed to me final and devastating. The driver snapped the reins and the horses lurched and found their footing in the mud, even though they dragged the coach for several yards before its wheels caught and began to turn. The coach and the seven dark hunched figures passed the far corner of the yard into the trees, and that was the last I saw of my father.

The next morning, I went down to the kitchen, where my mother was making pancakes. I sat at my place at the table and noticed there was no setting for my father. I usually sat on his left and my mother, when she sat to din-ner (she never sat with us at breakfast), ate across from him at the other end of the table. I said, Where is Dad? My mother paused in her cooking, spatula in one hand, the other holding the handle of the iron skillet wrapped in a dish towel. Howard, she said, Father is gone. The win-dows in the kitchen all faced west, so they allowed the morning light into the room only as it was reflected from the last clouds receding with the darkness and from the trees at the edge of the woods beyond the yard. It seemed to me that this was a dream of my father's death, a sort of rehearsal for when it really happened, rather than a sim-ple fact of the waking world. It was difficult for me to dis-tinguish the actual from dreaming during that time, because I often had dreams in which my father came into my bedroom to kiss me and cover me up with my blankets, which, restless sleeper that I was, had fallen to the floor. In those dreams, I awoke and, seeing my father, felt an over-whelming sense of how precious he was to me. His hav-ing died once, I understood what it would mean to lose him, and now that he had returned I was determined to take better care of him. Dad, I said to him in those dreams, what are you doing here? I'm not gone just yet, he would tell me in a humorous tone that I should have recognized as belonging to a dream, since he had never used it in life, although I had often wished for it. Well, this time we're going to make sure you stay well, I would say, and hug him.

But what, scurrilous babbler? Shall your barren wind slake the flame burning within my own heart? By no means! For mine is the flame that does not consume, and the guff from your bellows shall only fan it, that it burns all the brighter, the hotter, and the more surely.

I decided to try to find my father in the woods. When I walked through the woods, I wore my father's old boots. They were too large, so I had to put on three pairs of socks to make them snug. I carried my lunch in his old wicker creel, slung over my shoulder. I wore his wide-brimmed hat. When I walked through the Gaspars' corn patch, I imagined breaking an ear from its stalk, peeling its husk, and finding my father's teeth lining the cob. They were clean and white, but worn like his. Strands of my father's hair encased the teeth instead of corn silk.

As I hiked through the woods, I imagined peeling the bark from a birch tree, the outer layers supple, like skin. I would peel until I came to the wood. I would insert the tip of my knife into the wood and force the blade deeper until it touched something hard. I would cut a seam in the wood, prying it open an inch at a time, and find a long bone encased in the middle of the trunk. I imagined pulling flat rocks up from creek beds. I imagined climbing trees and tasting for traces of my father in their sap. This is how I thought of myself, as looking for what he had always called in his sermons the deep and secret yes, an idea I never knew whether was his own or something he had read in his books. I roamed the different places that we had gone together, but soon found myself hiking toward the outlet of Tagg Pond.

Spring rain made temporary ponds of the deep ruts along the abandoned tote roads. The water was shin-deep and the color of iron cream. Howard had to walk through one sometimes because it extended across the width of the entire road and into the woods. As he waded through, his feet pushed up milky, rust-colored clouds of mud from the bottom, out of which spurted schools of bright green tadpoles disturbed in their rapid and fragile evolutions. The tom-tom tap of a pileated woodpecker sounded from somewhere in the woods, to Howard's left. He thought of leaving the road to find it but decided not to. Grass covered the raised spine of the road where it was not submerged in the metallic water. Howard walked along this narrow path. The road originally had been more or less straight, but, once abandoned, the woods had shifted it over the years, canting lengths of it to the left or right, skewing it and encircling it above, so that walking down it was like walking through a tunnel. Light filtered down from the sky in various amounts. The branches of maples and oaks and birch leaned across the road toward one another and intertwined and became nearly indistinguish-able, their leaves mixed up, apparently sharing common branches, as if, after so many mingled seasons, the trees had grafted into one another and become a single plant that produced the leaves of several species. The light was trapped above Howard's head, glittering and abundant. Very few drops of it made their way through the tangle and into the grass. Howard twice passed places where the light gushed down and pooled over the ground—once where a giant blighted oak tree stood and then farther on, where lightning had split a huge spruce.

What looked like the end of the road was, in fact, merely a shift to the left or the right or a dip or gradual rise. And the way the clouds moved, mostly invisible, above the canopy of trees, now revealing the full light of the sun, now obscuring it, now diffusing it, reflecting it, and the way it sparkled and trickled and gushed and flooded and spun, and the way the wind dispersed it even more among the flickering leaves and twitching grass, all combined to make Howard feel as if he were walking through a kaleidoscope. It was as if the sky and the ground were turning end over end in front of him, around in a circle, so that the earth, as it swung up over the sky, dropped leaves and spears of grass and wildflowers and tree branches into the blueness and, as it rolled back down toward its proper place, in turn, received a precipitation of clouds and light and wind and sun from the sky. Sky and earth were now where they belonged, now side by side, now inverted, and now righted again in one seamless, silent spinning. Heedless animals picked their way through this turning thicket; birds and dragonflies dropped onto twigs and took off again for the skies; foxes padded over clouds and stepped back onto the forest floor without a pause; and thousands of tadpole tails flickered down from the watery ceiling and then sank back to their muddy nests. The light, too, shattered like a vast plate and rejoined itself and splintered again, shards and chips and glowing glass and backlit wisps of it turning in hushed and peaceful exchange and saturating everything Howard saw, so that all things themselves finally seemed to dissolve away and their shapes be held by nothing more than quills of colored light.

Howard eventually comes to the outlet at Tagg Pond. The day is unusually warm. He stoops to examine how the water has arranged silt and leaves around the stones in the pools beyond the first reaches of the outlet. The silt and water combine in an element that is half earth and half liquid. The appearance is that of a solid streambed. Howard takes off his father's boots and the three pairs of socks he is wearing and rolls up the legs of his pants. When he steps into the water, the mud yields, a phantom floor that gives way to the true ground with little more resistance than the water flowing over it. Howard's legs stir the silt into clouds, so he stands still for a time, watching a pair of cedar waxwings catch insects over the water and return to the same branch on a juniper bush growing on a hump of grass in the middle of the pool. The clouds of silt unfurl and the current carries them away. Then the water in which he stands is clear again and his legs look as if they end at the knees. The sunken halves of his legs stand buried in the silt among hidden branches and stones, which, because they are invisible, feel somehow like bones. After a time, small brook trout return to where he stands near the high grass and bushes of the bank. Clusters of frog eggs float past him, some close enough to see the embryos inside. Howard traces the riverbed with his feet and finds a flat stone broad enough to sit on. He finds another stone to place in his lap, so that the water will not lift him. He sinks down into the silt and sits on the flat stone. The silt is so deep where the stone is that only his head rises above the water and only his neck rises above the silt. He watches the silt billow away from his neck, as if his severed head has been tossed on the water and, rather than blood, bleeds clouds of soil.

It is now the middle of the afternoon and Howard

decides to sit this way through the entire night, until the sun rises the next morning. By the time the shadows begin to lengthen and creep across the water, the stream has healed itself back around him and he imagines that he will now be able to see the animals and the light and the water the way they are when he is not present, and that that might tell him something about his father. I will have to sit still, like a guru, he thinks. I will have to ignore cramps and the cold. I have to breathe very slowly and very quietly, so that my breath does not even stir the water flowing past my chin. I have to ignore whatever slithers past me in the mud. I cannot fall asleep. I am bound to see frightening things. What if I see lights in the sky? What if I see shadows sprinting through the tops of the trees? What if I see wolves walk on two feet and crouch like men to drink from the stream? What if there is a storm? What if it is clear and the sky brimming so full of stars that the light overflows down onto the earth and transforms into luminescent white flowers along the bank, which sparkle and disperse without a trace the moment the planet passes the deepest meridian of night and begins turning back toward the sun? What if I see my father, just inside the trees, humming softly to himself, content and at peace until he notices me sitting in the mud?

Sometime after midnight, I saw another head on the water, partially obscured by the grass overgrowing the bank, several yards downstream, just before the pool turned into a brook and turned east. The moon was bright and it illuminated the head. The head faced me. I tried to see its eyes, which I knew were open and were staring at me without blinking, but when I looked straight at them, my vision inked over. It was only by looking to the left or right of them that they became clear, or at least clearly eyes, which I imagined were open and staring. It was an Indian. He had not been there when I sat down in the water. I had not seen him arrive, even though we faced each other. Somehow, I knew that I could not move, that something terrible might happen if I did. I regretted coming to look for reliquaries of my father, at the foolishness of the act. It seemed to me then that my father had been a man of steady and real faith and that I was a foolish, lonely, miserable child. The night passed and the Indian did not move, except for once, when a small trout leapt from the water and down his throat.

I thought that the Indian must be Old Sabbatis. Sabbatis had grown up living on an island in the lake before he went to live with Red in his cabin. He worked as a fishing and hunting guide. Usually, he wore a flannel shirt and pants held up with white suspenders and a floppy wide-brimmed hat. The only traditional part of his costume was his moccasins, which he made himself. Some sportsmen were clearly disappointed when they first saw him, their fantasies of being led through the woods by an Indian clearly having conjured a more exot-.

ic image. Once a year, though, Sabbatis put on an old headdress and buckskin leggings and beaded vest, bought and kept for him by J. T. Saunders, and good naturedly, we thought, played the part of Indian chief in Saunders's display down at the Boston Sportsmen show.

But the head on the water did not look like Sabbatis. Its stillness could have been Sabbatis'. I had often heard stories of sportsmen leaving him at camp early in the morning, after he had made them breakfast, sitting in a certain position, facing a certain direction, and returning several hours later to find him in the same place. He always rose, though, the moment the men returned, and took whatever fish or small game they had caught and began preparing lunch, joking about how all of the big fish must have been hiding from the white men. But this was a different stillness. It seemed terrible, nearly inhuman. When the head's mouth opened, almost before the fish had even broken the surface of the stream, it made a hole, into which the dark water smoothly flowed. Although the head was far away, I was certain I heard the echo of the water funneling down its throat in the instant before the fish leapt. When the fish leapt, it was not like the normal rise of a fish striking a mayfly; the fish, unlikely, impossible, invisible itself, its existence only traced by the water from which it emerged, jumped directly down the Indian's throat. It did not struggle. It did not thrash its tail against any teeth, nor did it worry with the tongue, which might possibly have seemed to it like another fish. It simply dived straight down the open throat, with the mouth closing behind it so quickly that the whole event seemed as if it hadn't actually happened outside of my imagination. In fact, it seemed not to happen at all, but, rather, suddenly, to have happened.

The Indian's face was as it had been before.

Then the face was my own. For an instant, the Indian's face turned to mine and I was looking at myself, as if in a mirror. I noticed the very first light of the day in the tops of the trees. There was a sudden breath of wind and I felt sore and so cold, I thought I might lose consciousness. The head in the water was gone. I could not have looked away for more than an instant, certainly not enough time for the Indian to have risen from the water and disappeared into the woods. The water was undisturbed, too; there wasn't a trace of any body entering or leaving it. My dismay at the head's disappearance is the last thing I remembered before waking up slung in a canvas tent and being carried out of the woods by Ed Titcomb and Rafe Sanders, who had come upon me while hunting and found me, passed out half in and half out of the water in the outlet. The canvas smelled like fish guts and stale smoke and old rain. He's not dead, I guess, Rafe said when he saw my eyes open. He was at my head, Ed at my feet. Should be, Ed said without turning. Rafe's face was directly above me, it and the trees behind it swinging in rhythm to Rafe's and Ed's steps. Their progress was quick but awkward and I am certain they would have preferred to carry me lashed to a birch pole by my wrists and ankles, the way they carried the bears that they shot. Rafe was smoking a cigarette, as always. Might still yet, he said. The ash sagging from his cigarette exploded like a burst of confetti when he said the *s* in still and it spun down into my hair and onto my face. I looked forward and saw Ed's stooped back covered by his red flannel shirt. His hat covered his wavy black hair but his head was bent forward and his pale neck visible. I thought, He'll be chewing his tobacco, too, and just before I lost consciousness again, I saw a jet of tea-colored juice spurt from his hidden face into the brush alongside the trail.

I remember that my father had a birch canoe when I was very young. Indians made the canoe and my father bought it from them. Every spring, when the ice went out, one of the Indians would appear out of the woods one morning and restore the canoe for the season. I never saw my faher speak with the Indian and I do not know how payment was made or collected or in what currency it was paid. After resewing loose seams and inserting new bark where it was needed, the Indian simply disappeared back into the trees. I remember squatting in the grass several yards from where the Indian worked, trying to learn what I might, which was nothing, but still something I felt compelled to do, as if my lesson was no more than the effort I made. After glancing away for a moment to look at the first robin of spring, I looked back at the canoe and the Indian had vanished without sound, without, seemingly, even movement, but, rather, had been reabsorbed back not only into trunk and root, stone and leaf but into light and shadow and season and time itself.

It may have been Old Sabbatis who repaired my father's canoe every spring, not long after the ice had gone out of the ponds and lakes. He seemed to me as old as light and just as diffuse. I thought about him when the sky filled with files of dark clouds, whose silhouettes were traced by the sun and which were interspersed with the clearest and cleanest blue imaginable. When gold and red and brown leaves blow across paths and are taken up by circles of wind, it seems like the passing of his time. When new buds light up wet black branches, they seem to burst forth from another side of time, which belonged to Sabbatis and men like my father. Of course, Sabbatis is ancient only to me. My father is ancient, too, because both were men who passed from life when I was young. My memories of them are atmospheres. Old Sabbatis was used to scare children or to explain strange weather. Sometimes he was seen in the tops of trees. Sometimes men on the lake saw him dart by in the water deep beneath their boats, chasing salmon. Old Red was famously silent about Sabbatis. Men who used him as a guide regularly asked Red about him and Red would say only that Sabbatis was gone. Even the older men who had used

Sabbatis himself as a guide before, the year being sometime around 1896 or 1897—no one could agree; it was
somehow just understood that Red was now the guide
for fishing and hunting trips—even they would not talk
about him, deepening an impression of a nearly prehis-
toric era, when hunting must have been far more
dangerous and brutal, not the least for being orches-
trated by a still half-wild Indian, who was old enough to
remember his own grandfather's stories of raids not on
bear or deer but on men, and who, for that reason, was
closely watched and quarantined from the supply of rye
and whiskey while on any expedition, in case the spirits
should spark some atavistic fury. None of these older
white men doubted for a moment that the Indian could
slaughter a party of eight or ten armed men should he
avail himself of his forefathers' savage wisdom. And,
from the talk of theirs I heard when I was a boy, none of
them thought for a moment that he actually ever would
scalp a party in its sleep or as it was spread out through
the woods on a hunt, although none of them seemed to
mind that the more they protested Sabbatis' pacific
nature, the more people seemed convinced that these
men had somehow undertaken to set up camp with the
devil himself, and that sleeping and hunting under his
direction for weeks on end in the wilderness and coming home afterward, unscathed, to their jobs as bankers
and lawyers and managers at the mills was a sign of their
deep and true faith and nearly heroic strength of char-

acter, and they themselves eventually came to seem men who stood astride the old world of fire and flood and the new one of production quotas and commodities markets.

Of course, Sabbatis was a man, like any other. It was known that he liked looking at any photographs people were willing to show him, although he refused to have his own taken, unless, strangely enough, it was with a baby. Several photos exist of him standing on the front gallery of Titcomb's general store or on the porch of the North Carry Hotel (where he worked for many summers cutting wood) with a child held in the crook of his arms. These were the only times Sabbatis was known to have smiled. He also had a fondness for saltwater taffy, which he regularly accepted as part of his payment for acting as a guide from sportsmen who came up from Boston. He had no teeth and simply slid a stretch of the candy between his gums and his cheek and let it dissolve. He and Red, who was called Little Red in those days, lived in a cabin just beyond town, behind where Gooding street was made and houses put up for the new managers of the mills, who were hired in anticipation of the increase in business when the trains came through West Cove. No one knew whether Sabbatis and Red were related by blood. Some of the old librarians, who had a sense of the town's history, thought they might be distant cousins, and could easily be provoked into heated arguments about the matter during a slow winter

twilight at the checkout desk in the library. It may simply be that Sabbatis and Red lived together because it
was better to them to live with even the strangest Indian
than the friendliest white man. They were rarely seen
together outside of their yard and were never heard
speaking with each other at all. Little Red became Old
Red only when Sabbatis died, or disappeared, as the
case was. In the fall of 1896 or 1897, depending on who
was asked, men came to the cabin to arrange for the season's hunting trips, and Sabbatis was not there. Red said,
He's gone, and that was that. Red seemed to understand
the disappointment of the men—that he was somehow
more tame and domesticated than his predecessor. So,
Old Red took the men on their trips and did just as well
as Sabbatis had, with apparently neither training nor
experience. In becoming Old Red, he seemed to relin-
quish himself as a particular man and become the
embodiment of some eternal thing that itself stood outside of time and whose existence as any given person
was merely circumstantial.

Ed and Rafe did not want to miss out on a good day's
hunting, perhaps because their families depended on it,
and they must have decided that I was in no danger of
perishing because they dropped me off at the junction
of two tote roads, where, they knew, a lumber crew
would pass sometime that morning. I must have wakened at some point and wandered back into the woods.

This is when I believe I had my first epileptic seizure. When I awoke again, I spent some time lost and I did not return home until after the sun had set. I was wet and chilled through. Blood caked my hair and had run in a line from the corners of my mouth, down along my jawline, and into my ears, where it had collected and thickened. Even though I could hear my own panting as I made my way through the dark, I thought I had gone deaf because I couldn't hear anything outside of me, like my own footsteps or the wind. My tongue was swollen so much from my nearly biting it off that I could not properly close my mouth.

When I entered the kitchen through the back mudroom, my mother was sitting at the kitchen table mending a pair of my socks. She said something to me without looking up or even moving her mouth. This was the way she usually addressed me. There was no reason for her to raise her voice or look me in the eye or say my name, for that matter, in order to get my attention. She and I expected that I would simply always heed her words.

I shouted back to her, I had a spell and went deaf.

She put down her needle and thread and came and took me by the hand and led me to the table. She sat me down and went out to the pump, where she soaked a towel. I could smell the plain soap she used, and the wood burning in the stove, and the food smell of the kitchen, which was vaguely like chicken and butter and bread, although she had not cooked any dinner.

First, she scrubbed the blood out of my ears. The sounds of the world hissed in my head, clearer than I remembered them.

I said you are in a state, she said.

I went looking for Dad.

Then she scrubbed the blood from my face and hair. My skin stung from how hard she scrubbed and it seemed she would pull my hair right from my scalp. She wept as she cleaned me. She did not sob, but must have muted her grief by cleaning me so fiercely that I finally yelped, and she calmed. She took my face in her hands, which were cold and raw and calloused, and told me to open my mouth.

You must not speak for a week.

I began to say, No, I went looking for Father's teeth in tree wood and his hair in the stalks of bushes and— but she clamped my face more tightly and said, Stop. Seven days. Your tongue will fall off if you speak any more. It may have been true, for all I ever knew. It felt forked in my mouth, odd, mangled. I didn't dare to look at it in the mirror.

This was the first night my mother and I spent together in the kitchen without my father, she mostly at the stove preparing food or in the straight chair by the woodstove mending our clothes. On Sunday nights, she ironed the sheets and the curtains and I did my home-work to the sound of the hissing steam and the smell of scorched starch. Long after my tongue healed and I was able to speak, my mother and I remained silent.

That first night, however, she made a broth and fed it to me through a tin basting wand, which she inserted into my mouth along the side and down to the back, nearly into my throat, in order not to touch my tongue, like a mother bird feeding a chick. The broth was very hot and salty and it scalded its way down to my stomach. Once its heat was inside me, it radiated out from my middle, until I was finally warmed through. My mother was very patient. The process took nearly an hour. I recall only the gradual exchange of coldness and pain for warmth and exhaustion. The forest had nearly wicked from me that tiny germ of heat allotted to each person and I realized then how slight, how fragile it was, how it almost could not even be properly called heat, as its amount was so small and whatever its source so slight, and how it was just like my father disappearing or the house, when seen from the water, flickering and blinking out.

4

DURING THE DAYS, GEORGE WAS AWARE OF A large group of people murmuring and flowing in and out of the room as if on tides. At night, though, when he awoke, there was only and always one person sitting on the couch next to his bed, reading by the dim light of a small pewter lamp set on the rolltop desk at the far end of the couch. The person was always familiar to him, but he never knew exactly who it was—if the person was a man or woman, relative or friend. It was as if every time he tried to gather his senses and focus on the person—hair, eyes, cheekbones, nose—in order to recall a name, the person retreated to his peripheral vision, this even though the person remained sitting in full view.

The first night he found the benevolent stranger, he asked, Who are you? And the person looked up from the book and smiled and said, You are awake. He asked,

What time is it? The person answered, It is very late. This exchange seemed to occur without him or the person speaking. George could not tell if it was the pills or his normal confusion or if, in fact, he and the person were even communicating at all. It seemed even that when he wondered this to himself, the person answered, You are right here, speaking with me. You are as clear as a chime.

George attempted to see the person clearly by looking away for a moment and concentrating on the still-life painting at the opposite end of the room and then looking back, concentrating on trying to look straight into the person's eyes. When he did this, the person seemed like a will-o'-the-wisp, seemed not to sit on the couch, but to hover just above its cushions, and, whenever looked at, to dart to the left or right, up or down, without apparent conscious effort, as if the movement was a reflex, some natural defense, so that instead of being observed directly, he or she always presented an elusive vision flickering against a background of curtain, lamp, desk, couch.

The person was young—not a child, not an adolescent, but much younger than George's eighty years, at least in body; the person radiated a sense of possessing hundreds of years, but as a simultaneity: The person contained hundreds of years, but they overlapped, as if the person experienced any number of times at once.

I was just thinking, the person said in a silvery voice,

I was just thinking that I am not very many years old, but that I am a century wide. I think that I have my literal age but am surrounded in a radius of years. I think that these years of days, this near century of years, is a gift from you. Thank you. Now, let me read you something to get you back to sleep.

Cometa Borealis: We entered the atmosphere at dusk. We trailed a wake of fire. We were a sparkling trail of white fire hurtling over herds that grazed alluvial plains. The purple plains: steppe and table, clastic rocks from an extinct river strewn over the bed of an extinct ocean. Perhaps, far away, there was a revolution—the storming of a bereft fort built on the bend of a remote, misty, woods-shrouded river. But here only heavy-coated caribou lifted their shagged heads, their velvet antlers, not even stopping their chewing while our silent blazing passed across the cold sky, followed by their wet black eyes, but only because that is the nature of eyes and of light. Winds swept over the plains. We never saw the caribou or the revolution. We were a burning fuse. We barely caught a glimpse of the darkening world below us before we burned away to nothing.

Seventy-two hours before George died, Nikki Bocheki, an old acquaintance from the Unitarian church, showed up in a red Alfa Romeo convertible and flowing scarves.

She took off her large sunglasses and kissed George's wife on each cheek. When she saw George in his bed, she said, Oh George, you handsome thing! She kissed him on the forehead and her lips left a livid lipstick print. George did not recognize her but made a silly face like a cartoon character. And who's this beautiful lady? he said, which was just the right thing to say, even though he said it not only to be charming but also because he did not actually know. Nikki put a hand on his shoulder, called him an incurable gentleman, and blushed.

Nikki was an old woman who dressed like an aging former starlet whose most dramatic, and final, role was that of the aging former starlet persevering under the tyranny of time. She was, in fact, a nurse. Once she had chatted with George (who never remembered who she was) and his wife, she shooed the exhausted family from the room. I have three hours before my shift and I can't think of a nicer way to spend it than taking care of this sweetie pie. May I have a razor and a towel and some hot water? It isn't right that George doesn't have a good shave; he always dressed so smartly. He always looked so dapper.

When the family returned two hours later from their naps and furtive cigarettes and whispered arguments in the side yard, Nikki was sitting next to George, reading a glossy magazine called *International Luxury Properties* and chewing a stick of sugarless gum. George lay asleep beneath a white sheet, with only his head visible. His face was clean and smooth, his hair trimmed and combed. He wore his glasses. He looked as if he had fallen asleep in a barber's chair. When the family said what a lovely job she had done, Nikki said, Oh, yes, yes, well you know, all we have is our looks.

The escapement on a clock consists of a collar on a pinion, called a pallet, and an escape wheel, located at the top of the clock's works. It is placed at the end of the going train. The going train is that part of the clock which keeps time. If a clock has chimes, there is also a striking train. The striking train powers and regulates the clock's striking mechanism, which most simply consists of a gathering pallet, a mallet, and a coiled length of steel, which, when struck by the mallet, produces a chime. Each of these trains is powered by a spring. The spring, or mainspring, is a long spiral- shaped ribbon of flattened steel. The spring is attached at its end that is the innermost of the spiral to an arbor. This arbor is turned with a key to wind the clock; that is, to wind the spring. The spring is kept from unraveling during winding by a click wheel and ratchet pawl. In later clocks, it is housed in a brass drum called the spring barrel. The mainspring then unwinds and the power thus released is transferred to a series of wheels and gears, which move the minute and hour hands around the dial of the clock.

At the end of this train is the escapement. This is where the energy generated by the mainspring finally escapes the clock. It is also where the clock's regularity of beat is maintained; so we have returned to the pallet and escape wheel. The power comes through the escape wheel, which, being at the end of the going train, is the finest, most elegant and sensitive of the wheels. It bids the power, which has been tamed by the successive gears from savage energy to civilized servant, to perform the most rarefied of tasks: namely, to cooperate with the pallet to mark precisely each of the 86,400 seconds in our earthly day, and, furthermore, to do so for eight days at a time, making for a total of 691,200 seconds, or 192 hours. This cooperation, and each of these hundreds of thousands of seconds, may be heard at our leisure as the calming, reassuring tick-tocks of a winter's night from the bracket clock on the mantel above the glowing fire. If we call roll through the years, Huygens, Graham, Harrison, Tompion, Debaufre, Mudge, LeRoy, Kendall, and, most recently, Mr. Arnold, we find a humble and motley, if determined and patient, parade of reasonable souls, all bent at their worktables, filing brass and calibrating gears and sketching ideas until their pencils dissolve into lead dust between their fingers, all to more perfectly trans*form* and trans*late* Universal Energy by perfecting the beat of the escape wheel. Listen, horologist, to the names of their devices: verge, dead-beat, tic-tac, gridiron, grasshopper, rack lever, gravity, détente, pinwheel. Like our greatest bards, those manly and sensitive souls who range over hill and through wood, who ponder the sheep grazing among the ancient ruins and there find rhyme and meter; in short, find the music of sweetest verse, so, too, our greatest clock men find that poetry resides in the human process of distilling civilization from riotous nature! Welcome, fellow, welcome!

—from *The Reasonable Horologist*,
by the Rev. Kenner Davenport, 1783

Family and close friends never knocked before entering George's house and they always came in by the back door, through the three-season porch, and into the kitchen. George would either be in the basement working on clocks, napping on the couch in the living room (his forearm over his head, his glasses on the coffee table), or, if it was lunchtime, sitting at the kitchen table, looking at the *Wall Street Journal* and complaining to his wife that the meal was taking too long, to which she would respond, Oh, shut up and make it yourself if you want it so fast. He and his wife often bickered like this. He would complain about her cooking (which was very good) or his laundry (which she not only did but also ironed every piece of, including his

undershirts and briefs) and she would bellow back that
he could go to hell if he didn't like it and that she was
going shopping for shoes. They'd both laugh then. So
the house smelled of starch and laundry detergent and
roast chicken and linseed oil and brass. Visitors appearing in his living room and waking him from his light
sleep never startled George. (Even at night, as he snored
uproariously, the quietest word would rouse him to
complete wakefulness.)

Customers dropping off or picking up clocks came
to the front door, which was located in a small entryway
attached to the living room. By the time of his final illness, George's wife had tired of her days being constantly
interrupted by strangers appearing with black marble
mantel clocks in cardboard boxes, walnut schoolhouse
clocks tucked under their arms, or decrepit long-case
clocks lashed to handcarts and wheeled up the walk. She
also tired of George's way of talking with his customers,
a combination of easy, joking familiarity and conspira-
torial regret. She became especially uncomfortable when
the customers pulled out their checkbooks and asked
what they owed. The price always seemed to surprise, if
not actually anger them. When he had few or no customers scheduled to come to the house, George often
spent the day driving all over the North Shore and Cape
Ann, redeeming checks at the banks from which the
funds were drawn, so that all of his deposits to his own
accounts were made in cash. He also kept safety-deposit

boxes at six different banks, which he worked at filling with one-hundred-dollar bills. By the time of his dying, there were these six boxes of cash, another full of treasury bills, three checking accounts, two savings accounts, and seven certificates of deposit tucked away in a total of eight different banks. George regularly visited each bank in order to soothe himself with rates and principals, compound interest and tightly banded stacks of bills.

George most often visited with Edward Billings, the manager of the Enon branch of the Salem Five bank. Edward stood a foot and a half higher than George, like a fleshy Olympian pear trussed up in a three-piece suit. Even his head seemed tall and elongated. It was topped by a bald dome, which reflected the ceiling lights of the bank so clearly that it seemed lit from within. The band of hair circling the circumference of his head was meticulously dyed, and when he did not have his hands pressed to each other at the tips of his fingers, as if in a kind of prayer or exhortation, he smoothed it down along the back of his skull with the end of a middle finger. The two looked like a vaudeville act one Tuesday morning in January, standing next to each other behind Edward's desk at the back of the bank, looking at the especially large Vienna regulator clock hung on the wall. George maintained the clock for Edward (at the bank's expense, of course), and the two contemplated the motionless pendulum as they spoke.

Damn thing just stopped, Mr. Crosby, Edward said.

George said, These things are tricky bastards. George saw, with his years of experience, that the clock had been merely brushed off level by the enormous banker as he had inserted or extracted himself behind his desk, and that the pendulum would therefore run down and stop ten minutes after whenever it was started. Edward's phone rang and he excused himself to answer it. He spoke with his head bowed and his back turned to George. As he told a Mr. White on the other end of the line that, yes, he'd have those summaries by the end of the week, George righted the clock on the hook from which it hung. Edward turned back toward George and held up an index finger and nodded to him, saying into the phone, Yes, yes, that's right, Friday at the latest, Saturday morning at the very latest, if the Lynn branch can't hop to it. George nodded back and mouthed, I have to go out to the car.

George brought a stepladder and a tackle box full of tools back into the bank. He set the ladder up in front of the clock, opened its large glass door, mounted the ladder, and peered up into the clock. He grunted and swore and dismounted the ladder to change tools three times, all while thinking of his children and his grand-children, their winter clothes and their new roofs, their failing transmissions and foundering marriages, their fifth years at private colleges. At the end of half an hour, he finally said, Aha, I got you, you little son of a— And he climbed down the ladder, dabbing his forehead with a handkerchief. Edward filled out a yellow form and drew three one-hundred-dollar bills from one of the tellers' drawers, which George promptly handed back to the teller, a middle-aged woman named Eddie, who had worked at the bank since it had opened in 1961, and told her, Just put these in that little gray box I have out back, my dear, along with all the others. How did I ever know you were going to say that, Mr. Crosby? she said, laughing and making her chewing gum pop. She took the bills and licked her thumb and snapped each one twice, counting, One two three, One two *three*, and buzzed herself into the bank's vault. At that moment, the bank, quiet and ordered, bland music quietly burbling overhead from the speakers in the ceiling, seemed to George bathed in a golden light.

The wallpaper in George's basement workroom had a pattern of larch branches on a dunn-colored background. Clocks in various states of repair and disrepair hung on wall, some ticking, some not, some in their cases, some no more than naked brass works fitted with their pairs of hands. Cuckoos and Vienna regulators and schoolhouse and old railroad station clocks hung at different heights. There were often twenty-five or thirty clocks on the wall. Some of them were clocks he wanted to sell. None was marked. The closet to the left of his desk was made from raw pine planks and took up the space beneath the stairway. Between the pine planks and the arboreal wall-paper and the wood of the clocks, and the fact that the only windows were two small dry wells high in the wall near the ceiling, one felt one was in some odd, ticking bower. George sat at his desk at all hours of the day, looking down through his bifocals and often through one or two lenses of a clip-on set of jeweler's loops down into the brass guts of clocks, pushing and pulling at arbors and gears and ratchets, humming non-existent melodies, which evaporated as he unconsciously composed them. In this setting, he drove numerous fidgety grand-children to near madness, insisting that they sit in a hard chair and watch him hum and poke around to no appar-ent effect. This is the thing to get into, boy. I tell you, this is how you can make some *bucks*. There was little to do but try to pick out recognizable bits of songs from his humming, which none of the children could do, and listen to the way that the tickings of the different clocks, which not only lined the walls but were also crowded onto several folding card tables, an old cot, and the shelves of a built-in bookcase, fell into and out of beat with one another. On rare occasions, every clock in the room seemed to tick at the same time. By the next tock, however, they all began to drift away from one another again and George's hapless victim would nearly weep at the prospect of having to sit still and listen again for the confluence. The only light in the room was one small wall lamp fitted with a forty-watt bulb and George's fluorescent jeweler's lamp, which was clamped to the desktop and could be pulled into almost any conceivable angle in order to illuminate almost any depths the works of a clock might present. This light provided the only other source of diversion for the child condemned to witness the mysterious, agonizing, glacial, undramatic doings of antique clock repair: watching the dust float. The jeweler's lamp brilliantly lit the dust in the air near whatever clock was being worked on. The rest of the room was dark with clocks and the evergreen wallpaper and so provided a perfect contrast to the front-lit specks of dust that floated down into or across the lamp's halo. The child imagined the flecks were miniaturized ships exploring inner space: The giant is fixing the time machine. We can only hope he doesn't sneeze or make any sudden moves and create a vortex that will send us hopelessly off course. The ship is made only of lamb's wool and dander!

How to Make a Bird's Nest: Take a wafer of tinker's tin. With heavy scissors, cut four triangles. The triangles shall be small, no taller or wider than half an inch, preferably smaller, if possible. Punch holes near the two angles at the base of the triangle, using a small hammer and the slimmest nails or brads possible. A large, sturdy sewing needle is even better, as it will yield a finer hole. Fold each triangle along an imaginary line extending from the top point to the middle of the base. The angle of the fold should be as close to ninety degrees as possible, using only the naked eye (as the utility of the tool does not depend on exact mathematical measurement). Thread each of the pieces with a length of fishing line or kitchen string or strong sewing thread. Now, patience is required; place in turn each piece of shaped tin over the nails of the forefinger and thumb of each hand so that the end point of each piece extends approximately one-quarter of one inch beyond the fingertip. Fasten each piece to the finger by tightly tying the thread around the finger at the first joint (but not so tightly that circulation is lost). This may take practice. Join the thumb and forefinger at their pads. By rolling them together forward and back, the two folded triangles should variously meet and separate; these are your beaks. It is with these that you will pick up grass and twigs and tinsel and stray bits of string and weave them together in the branches of a chosen tree or bush or thicket, depending on the species whose nest you wish to undertake. (This in itself requires preparation and it is suggested that as many examples as possible of the desired type of nest be studied before attempting one's own version. Even more desirable is to spend as many a spring afternoon as manageable watching the birds themselves weave their homes; such observation will help immensely in learning the particular stitch required.) Keep in mind, though, that the materials for the nest must be col-

lected and woven *strand by strand*. Birds do not gather
their lumber, so to speak, all at once, but, rather, search
out each plank and shingle one at a time. Such a birdy
method may at first seem absurd to the forward-
thinking nest maker, but soon it will be found that the
pleasures of the project are not derived from efficiency.
(Another desired eventuality is that as one becomes
more and more dexterous weaving nests, one will begin
to do so with only one beak, as it were. And here, then,
too, is another temptation to overcome—keeping one's
free hand behind one's back and refraining from giving the birds a helping human hand!)

Once the nest is complete, then what to put in it?
Anything your heart desires, of course: acorn eggs
plucked from their cups; stones smoothed in a river; a
lock of your sweetheart's hair; your firstborn's milk
teeth—anything you choose that will fit into the nest and
give you pleasure to consider whenever you visit. Over
time, one's whole countryside might be fitted out with a
constellation of such nests, each holding its own special
treasure.

> —from a lost pamphlet by
> Howard Aaron Crosby, with
> accompanying illustrations and
> instructional diagrams, 1924

Howard entered North Philadelphia at seven in the
morning on a Saturday. By nine, he had sold his cart and

wares for twenty dollars and was a bag boy at the Great Atlantic and Pacific Tea Company. *The manager, Harry Miller, asked me my name and I thought, I stole the wagon and all of the supplies and sold it as my own, so my name is no longer Crosby, and I said to him, Lightman, Aaron Lightman, not sure if I should even keep my first name but not wanting to lose my name altogether, not wanting to cut the last thread, so I used my middle name, so here I lie on my bed next to my wife, not Kathleen Crosby, née Black, but Megan Lightman, née Finn, Aaron Lightman.* He started as a bag boy. He loved the job, the smell of the fresh coarse brown paper, the bundles of bags, sharp blocks of pulp, peeling bags off the piles, snapping them open. And he loved packing the bags—fitting boxes and jars and bottles and cans and the meat snugly in butcher paper, stringed tight, and fresh loaves of bread in their own bags. He took pride in fitting each bag like a puzzle, fitting the most items in that hollow rectangle of a cubic foot or two without making it too heavy for a woman to carry and balancing it perfectly so that the bag would not tear. The moment a woman began to pile her groceries on the checkout counter, Howard began to sort them and order them in his mind, so that by the time the crackers and the pot roasts and the sacks of flour were pushed his way, he already had them bagged in their neat brown wrappings and all that was left to do was embody those bags in his mind out of the actual apples and cans of lard and boxes of salt. Two months

after he was hired, he was promoted to head of the produce section and he made a paradise of fruit and vegeta-
bles. He made Thebes in oranges and lemons and limes.
He made primeval forests of lettuce and broccoli and
asparagus. He was enchanted by the smells of wax and
cold water and packing crates, of skins and rinds breath-
ing rumors of the sweet pulp beneath. In six months, he
was an assistant manager. He worked seven days a week
and wrote poems extolling his company over the compe-
tition (*The floor's a mess and I feel a dope, I scrubbed it down
with Red Lantern soap*). He married a woman named
Megan Finn who talked without pause from the moment
she woke—Well the good lord has given me another
day! shall I cook eggs and ham or flapjacks and bacon? I
have some blueberries left but those eggs will go bad if I
don't use them and I can put the blueberries in a cobbler
for dessert tonight because I know how much you love
cobbler and how the sugar crust soothes you to sleep like
warm milk does a crabby baby although I don't know
why because I saw somewhere that sugar winds a person
up but I'm not going to argue with what works—until
she went to sleep: Oh! Another day tucked away and
here we are tired and honest and in love and happy as
two peas in a pod, two peas in a pod! isn't that silly? peas
don't come in pairs! if they did it wouldn't be worth it
snapping them open, it'd take too long to even get a
spoonful never mind enough to fill from nine o'clock to
twelve o'clock, that's how the blind know where the food

is on their plates, like a clock, ham at six-thirty! biscuit at four! just like that, that's how Helen Keller did it, I bet, just like that, potatoes at high noon! goodnight my love.

Megan worked as a sorter in a canning factory. Well, I sort the beans and the peas and the carrots. . . . Oh, it's terribly hard and boring and you have to go so fast! In comes the asparagus and just like that I have to sort it by size, color, and quality into the different bins—and fast, fast, fast!—but it's for a good cause and canned food is better than fresh—I'm sorry, Mr. Produce Man!—because more vitamins get cooked away in the steam that comes out of the pot at home than when the wee peas are cooked right in the can. I know because they told us that they know that there are more vitamins in the canned peas because of all the experiments they do on white rats. It takes them five times as little canned food as fresh not to get scurvy!

Howard brought her flowers every day, and oranges. Each night before he left the store, he stopped in the produce section and lingered at the fruit bins, inhaling the clean smells of lemons and oranges, their citrus perfume. These sharp odors invigorated him. He lifted his nose from a crate of limes, refreshed and eager to get home to a wife who spoke words out loud as she thought them up and held nothing to whirl and eddy and collect in brackish silences, silences that broke like thin ice beneath you to announce your drowning.

*　*　*

George woke at night. He could barely speak. One of
his grandsons was sitting on the couch. He said his
wife's name, Erma. What, Gramp? Erma. No more
than a whisper, the name sounded remote in his
mouth. He could not shape the air, was unable to make
the first syllable with his tongue against his upper back
teeth, could only get the second syllable to work—ma
—so that it sounded as Uhma. Uhma. Water? Do you
want some water? Uhma. Erma? You want Nanny?
Uh. Uh. Yes.

His wife came from their bed, where she lay in
shallow sleep, alone, for a few hours each night as he
died. She wore a light blue cotton robe with darker
blue piping. Her slippers scuffed on the wood floor of
the hall because she walked with small steps and shuffled a bit with sleep and fatigue. The scuffing stopped
when she stepped onto the Persian rug covering the
living room floor. She stood by his head and leaned
down to him and stroked his face. Oh, George, you are
my heart's delight. Haven't we had a wonderful life
together? We've been around the whole world together.
She gave him a sip of water from a juice glass with
painted birds on it. The water helped his mouth and he
spoke. Who is reading to me? Who is reading? What is
that book? She said, What book, George? Have you
been reading to Gramp, Charlie? Charlie said, No,
Nan. She turned back to George and said, No one is
reading to you, George. George said, The big book.

No, my love, there is no book; no one is reading to you. There is no one here at all.

Howard had fewer seizures in Philadelphia. They still left him dazed, still left him feeling acrid and burned, as if an electric fire had swept through him. But afterward he enjoyed the cheerful ministrations of Megan. She led him to bed and rubbed his temples and gave him hot tea. Sometimes she read to him from one of her dime novels. The seizures did not upset her. She had read somewhere that they were considered holy in some cultures. Oh, my sweet, sweet Aaron, what an awful fit that was! I thought you'd break all of our finest china, the way all the cups and plates rattled in the cabinets. My goodness, you must feel terrible. Let's get you into bed and warm you up. What do you smell this time? Do you taste anything? I hope it's pork chops, because that's what's for dinner tonight, or apple pie, because I baked one this morning. I'm so glad there wasn't so much blood this time. You didn't bite your tongue at all, did you? That broomstick works so well. It's just the right size and I don't think you could ever bite through it. It looks like it's been chewed by a dog!

Eventually, she persuaded him to see a doctor, who prescribed bromides, which further lessened the frequency of the seizures. Lordy, I don't know what sort of witch doctors they have up in Canada, but here in the USA they are the best in the world. From the sounds of it, you were lucky they didn't shoot you like a dog with rabies. My dog, Mr. Jiggs, had rabies when I was a girl and he foamed at the mouth and stumbled in circles around the yard and my father rushed home from the mill with Charlie Weaver's shotgun and shot Mr. Jiggs dead right there on the spot and I cried for a week. He was such a free spirit! He chased all the boys and tore their pant cuffs and dug up all the neighbor's flower beds and ate a cat for dinner every day. Poor Mr. Jiggsy!

Domestica Borealis: 1. New Year's morning we watched crows collect tinsel for their nests from the discarded Christmas trees along the road. 2. We watched the leaded glass of our windows knit frost into lace. 3. We lashed fishing line to playing cards and raised a house. 4. After Sunday dinner we changed into our sackcloths and threw crab apples at our younger cousins. 5. We drew straws and flipped coins and played Chinese checkers. 6. When it came time to pick bedrooms, we arm-wrestled for choice. The winner chose the room resplendent with crowned kings, queens bestowing benedictions, mocking jokers, jacks with sly smiles. The loser was stuck with a more modest space of twos and fours and sevens, although we were all smitten with the glossy clubs and spades, the livid diamonds, the hearts so bloody red, they seemed nearly to beat.

George awoke for the last time forty-eight hours before he died. He had been unconscious for two days. This was when he understood the situation and needed to tell people things. There was $2,400 in cash hidden in his workbench downstairs. The Simon Willard banjo clock on the wall was worth ten times more than he'd ever told anyone. There was an inscribed first edition of *The Scarlet Letter* in a safety-deposit box. He loved everyone dearly.

He roused at a time when the last of his body's major systems had begun to stop. His lungs were full of liquid and he felt like he was drowning. When he tried to speak, he could only make noises that sounded like a rusted pulley turning over a dry well. He looked from person to person around his bed for help. This upset his family, particularly Marjorie, his sister, who cried and looked at his wide eyes and said over and over, He looks so *scared*. He was like my *daddy*, he looks so *scared*, he was like my *daddy*—until she was taken to the kitchen by one of the cousins. A grandson said, Just relax, Gramp, panicking just makes it harder to breathe. He gasped more, gasped faster. The grandson said, I know how it feels, Gramp; it happens when I get an asthma attack. I get scared, too, scared I can't breathe, but I just relax and I can always breathe. It happens to me, too. He looked at the young man, someone he knew and trusted. As his eyes closed, he still heard the gurgling and felt the nerveless weight of his body, but also felt himself falling away from it, as if he were lying just beneath the contours and boundaries of something that had formerly fit him perfectly, and which to fully inhab-it meant to be in this world. It was as if he lay faceup just beneath the surface of water. Voices rose and fell and the sounds of bodies in motion thumped above him. All seemed increasingly foreign, other. He just made out someone saying, No way, no way; I'm keeping him under now.

Choose any hour on the clock. It is possible, then, to conceive that the clock's purpose is to return the hands back to that time, a time which, from the moment chosen, the hands leave and skate across the rest of the clock's painted signs and calibrations and numbers. These other markings on the face become irrelevant in themselves; they are now simply clues pointing in the direction of the chosen time. It is then possible, too, to conceive of the clock's gears and springs as each having its own intrinsic function, but within a whole mechanism, the larger purpose of which is to return to the chosen time. In this manner, the clock resembles the universe. For is it not true that our universe is a mechanism consisting of celes-tial gears, spinning ball bearings, solar furnaces, all cooperating to return man (and, indeed, what other, unimagined neighbors of whom we are ignorant!) to that chosen hour we know of from the Bible as Before the Fall? And as an ignorant insect crawling across the face of that clock, who sees not the whole face, the full cycle of numbers, the short hand and the long (which pass in his sky with predictable orbits, cast familiar shadows, offer reassurance through their very repetitions, but which, ultimately, puzzle and beg for the consideration of deeper mysteries), but who merely treads over the surface which hides the gear train and the springs without any but the most indirect conception of what lies beneath, so does man squirm and fret on the dusty skin of our earth, ignorant of the purpose of the world, indeed, the cosmos, beyond the fact that there is one, assigned by God and known only to Him, and that it is good and that it is terrifying and that it is ineffable and that only rational faith can soothe the desperate pains and woes of our magnificent and depraved world. It is that simple, dear reader, that logical and that elegant.

—from *The Reasonable Horologist*,
by the Rev. Kenner Davenport, 1783

One January night in 1972, Howard's attention strayed from the book he was reading in bed. He imagined his own sleeping form, imagined that if one could pan back from peaceful face to bird's-eye view, one could see the supine figure floating not upon the vastness of a dark ocean of sleep but reposing in the vastation itself, the soul or whatever name one cared to give it divested of the body, so that what seemed reposing body was simply the most likely image of the whatever named soul, freed of its salt like seawater evaporating in the sun, so that the actual body, resting in bed, sighing, mumbling, came to be more like a scurf, more like that saline column of myth, while the soul or whatever one named it reattached itself in some way to the actual thing of itself like a shadow, as if when his waking self walked down the street on the way home from work, the shadow he made, of man with a paper bag holding six oranges under one arm and a small bouquet of lilies beneath the other, was some reduced version of himself, which, freed from its simple two dimensions defined by an obscurity of light, a projection of dark, would be autonomous and free to move independent of the silhouette cast by the man, and which, for all he knew, when the sun went down and the lamp was turned down, when all light, in fact, was removed from possibly coming between the body and the planes and surfaces upon which its form might be projected by sun, lamp, or even moon, actually did; he saw no reason to doubt that his shadow dreamed just as he did for the reason that he could imagine himself to be a shadow of something—someone—else and that perhaps even his sleep, his dreams, constituted his duty as a shadow of someone else and that perhaps while *that* someone else dreamed, he was free to live his waking life, so that this alternating, interdependent series of lives formed a sort of intaglio; the waking day of each shadow was the opposite side of its possessor's sleep. When he tried to explain this to Megan as they lay in bed, he with a copy of *The World's Book of Favorite Popular Verse* tented on his chest, she keeping her place in *The Poor Orphans of Tinsley Grange* with a forefinger, she said, That must be why you can't sleep some nights and have those awful nightmares about those big dark houses full of all those people you know but who don't recognize you, or that woman and her twin daughters frozen in the lake ice with all their long hair tangled up; your shadow wants a nap and so you have to get up so that it can sleep. Imagine that! And if your shadow wakes *you* up and you wake *me* up, my shadow must be taking a nap, too! Maybe our shadows are in cahoots, sweet pea; maybe they're partners in crime, just like us! Howard said, Maybe, my love. Maybe that is so, and he kissed Meg on the ear, closed his book, fell asleep, and died.

As George died, the dark blood retreated from his limbs. First, it left his feet, then his lower legs. Then it left his hands. He was aware of this only from a great distance. When the blood left, it was as if it had evaporated; it was as if the blood had turned to some fumy spirit too thin to carry its own minerals. And so, it evaporated and had left a residue of salt and metal along the passages of his dry veins. His bloodless legs were hard like wood. His bloodless legs were dead like planks. His bone-filled feet were like lead weights that were held by his dried veins—his salt-cured, metal-strengthened veins, which were now as tough as gut, as strong as iron chains. It was as if it would be possible to reach into his chest and grab the very vessels leading from his heart and pull at them and hoist the heavy bones of his feet up through his legs and trunk until they hung just below that nearly exhausted engine, and might, as their ponderous weight pulled at arteries and veins and they began to lower back down through his body, drive that worn-out organ just a little longer. But his heart was brittle and worn and out of beat. Its bushings were shot. It was caked in gummy scar. Now his blood trickled through its chambers with the weakest of ticks, whereas before it had flowed and eddied, tended, administered by supple and strong muscle.

His face was pale. It no longer showed expression. True, it showed a kind of peace, or, more precisely, seemed to predict that peace, but such peace was not a human one. It captured breath and let breath escape in fluttery little gasps and sighs. It no longer reacted to light. Shadows passed over it and it merely registered their angles, registered the pilgrimage of the day by their lengths. Certainly, George's family did not allow the direct glare of the rising or setting sun to fall upon his face, but their adjusting of curtain and shade was a palliative for themselves, for living eyes and living skin, and had nothing to do with the vision of their husband, brother, father, grandfather lying on the hospital bed.

Human consideration was no longer to be his, for that consideration could be expressed now only by providing physical comfort, and physical comfort was as meaningless to him (to it, for that was what lay before his family now—the it formerly he—at least to the extent that the he, although still figured by the struggling, fading, dying it, was plumbing depths far, far from that living room filled with a weeping sister and daughters and wife and grandchildren and the it merely maintaining a pantomime of human life), was as meaningless to him now as it would have been to one of his clocks, laid out in his place to be dusted and soothed with linseed oil, fussed over and mourned even before it was was (because that is how the living prepare, or attempt to prepare, for the unknowable was—by imagining was as it is still approaching; perhaps that is more true, that they mourn because of the inevitability of was and apply their own, human, terrors about their own wases to the it, which is so nearly was that it will not or simply cannot any longer accept their human grief) as its broken springs wound down or its lead weights lowered for the last, irreparable time.

Thought that he was a clock was like a clock was like a spring in a clock when it breaks and explodes when he had his fits. But he was not like a clock or at least was only like a clock to me. But to himself? Who knows? And so it is not he who was like a clock but me.

* * *

Two things happened in 1953: The new interstate highway opened and Howard's second wife's mother fell sick
in Pittsburgh. Megan told him he could not go with her
to Pittsburgh. Mother was the strictest of Catholics and
if she ever found out that her daughter was married to
the son of a Methodist minister, any chance she had of
recovering from her illness would vanish. Mother would
die with her mouth full of curses mingled with my
name, she said. This meant he had to spend Christmas
alone. Megan baked a banana cream pie and a meat loaf.
He walked her to the bus station and helped her onto
the four-thirty to Pittsburgh and all points between.
She talked the entire time. She opened the bus window
to tell him to take the vanilla ice cream out of the
freezer fifteen minutes before he had it with the pie,
that that made it soft, just like he liked it, and said, I love
you. He said, I'll be fine, I'll be fine, still baffled that she
had a mother in Pittsburgh. Twenty-five years she had a
mother in Pittsburgh.

Five months before, the interstate highway had been
finished. It ran in one long line up the eastern seaboard.
Immigrants, hobos, manual laborers pounded, carved,
blasted, and peeled the earth open through forests,
rivers, and gorges, mountains and swamps, then lined
the path with good clean gravel, filled it with piping-hot
blacktop, rolled it smooth, let it set to cool, and painted
a line down the middle. These new superhighways had
numbers for names. On the day before Christmas, he

put a cold meat loaf sandwich and six bottles of cola in a paper bag, along with his dopp kit, and called his friend from the A&P, Jimmy Drizos. He asked Jimmy if he could borrow his car, an old Ford sedan. Jimmy said, Sure, sure. The in-laws are coming here this year. Sure, sure you can, pal. He took a bus to Jimmy Drizos's house in the Greek part of town. Jimmy was replacing bulbs on strings of lights he had threaded around the iron handrails of the steps to his apartment. Jimmy offered him a drink. He said, No, thanks, Jimmy, no. Jimmy offered him some food to take back home. He said, Thank you, Jimmy, thank you and your wife. Jimmy gave him the keys and a plate of lamb and said, Easy on the clutch, pal. He nodded and pressed the clutch pedal and let the car roll out of the driveway, running in neutral. He shifted the car into first gear and let out the clutch as he pushed the gas pedal. Gears whirred, meshed, then jammed. The car lunged and stalled. Jimmy Drizos looked from his stairs, a colored Christmas bulb in each hand, and yelled, Whaddya', been drinking, pal? and laughed. Howard waved, got the car into gear, and crept away at five miles an hour until he reached the corner, drove over it, turned, and stalled again, this time out of Jimmy Drizos's sight. He spent four hours lurching through the streets of Philadelphia on Christmas Eve, teaching himself to drive. At nine o'clock in the evening, as a light snow started to fall, he drove Jimmy Drizos's Ford onto the highway heading north.

Megan's secret from him was that she had a mother in Pittsburgh. His secret from her was that he had tracked his first family and their migrations throughout New England. He had called post offices to confirm addresses. He called operators and was given new phone numbers. When his son George moved to Enon, Massachusetts, there were two G. Crosbys given by the operator. Howard called the first number. An old woman answered and said, This is Mrs. Gus Crosby. To whom am I speaking? Howard hung up and wrote the second number in his daybook.

Somewhere in Connecticut, he stopped and slept in the backseat of the Ford for four hours. He awoke freezing. He had stopped behind a gas station. He took his dopp kit and used the station bathroom. He brushed his teeth, combed his hair and ran a splash of tonic through it, and shaved with the straight-edge razor his father had given him when he was sixteen and which he still kept sharp enough to cut skin with only the weight of the blade. At noon, he left the highway at exit 24. He took a left and followed Main Street for three miles. He took another left onto Arbor Street and slowed, looking for street numbers on door frames and mailboxes. He came to a small yellow Cape Cod–style house with green shutters. The mailbox at the end of the flagstone walk leading to the front door read GEORGE W. CROSBY. Without turning the engine off, Howard got out of the car, walked up the walkway, and knocked on his son's front door.

Homo Borealis: 1. We kicked the bark off of dead trees and the soft wood beneath was as pale as sawdust and sometimes covered with strange designs that looked like writing that had been drawn into the wood with a stylus or fine-carving tool and the bark then fitted back over the trunk—a rough skin, a splintery hide that protected the secret language. These hieroglyphs we discovered like revelations, like messages someone had left for us alone to discover and to ponder and to poke and scratch at with our sticks but not to understand and to leave like totems for whomever they were actually meant while we crashed away through the bushes. 2. We made up stories about men who had been tattooed with intricate and important instructions. The tattoos were inked into deep layers and the men would be recognized by long, **I**-shaped scars on their backs, which would have to be recut and the skin opened like a pair of doors to reveal braids of muscle and the secret script. Of course, the men would not know that they were the bearers of these signs. And of course the people who were supposed to read these messages had to go through a very long and difficult process of deciphering obscure clues and directions in order to find these special couriers, in order to protect both the man and the message. The seeker would find the messenger; he would find himself recognizing the messenger as the messenger was trying to sell him an old horse, or serving him breakfast at an inn, or complaining about politicians during the morning coffee break. 3. Those stories were ignorant. We sensed, finally, the foolishness of attributing the unknown to secret cabals, to conspiracies. Everything was almost always obscure. Understanding shone when it did, for no discernable reason, and we were content. We built our town, then, out of whatever came our way, or whatever we got in the way of, so that we dwelled in huts of hair, in nests of wrappers and tinsel and string, which we looped through nuts and hung from the ceilings with a bit of tape or a piece of old gum because they all had different threads from the bolts we found. Town Hall was constructed of drinking straws (some with elbows, most not) and hubcaps and the foil from cigarette packages. Any number of people lived in the crooks of trees beneath tented Sunday newspapers, which were aged brown by the sun. When it rained, these buildings swelled and then turned to pulp and washed away and the tenants would dry themselves in the sun when it came back out and begin again to collect tin cans and nickels and matchboxes and greasy paper boats that had once held french fries or onion rings. 4. The green sea turned gray and its surface rolled like a membrane. When we dived for shells, it parted for us without resistance and sealed itself behind our up-pointed toes. We felt around, blind, in its slick graphite body, we sifted its sand and came up with smooth stones for our mantles of wind and mist, and whatever of it was held in our hair when we surfaced ran out like quicksilver and rejoined the rest of itself, seamless, molecular, slick, atomic. We traveled in pods. We breached surfaces and caught glimpses of sheer cliffs, columns of flint capped in fir, boreal. We saw beaches of snow and blizzards of sand. 5. When it came time to die, we knew and went to deep yards where we lay down and our bones turned to brass. We were picked over. We were used to fix broken clocks, music boxes; our pelvises were fitted onto pinions, our spines soldered into vast works. Our ribs were fitted as gear teeth and tapped and clicked like tusks. This is how, finally, we were joined.

The last thing George Washington Crosby remembered as he died was Christmas dinner, 1953. The doorbell rang just as he and his wife and two daughters—Betsy and Claire, the two daughters who now sat at his bedside haggard, pale, exhausted; the daughters he loved and whom he realized would be daddy's little girls as long as he allowed them, which was until the day he died, which was today—were sitting to eat. As he died, he did not remember getting up from the table and muttering, For Christ's sake, what is it now? and walking to the door. He remembered all of the time that stood between himself as a boy of twelve and himself as a middle-aged husband and father contracting to zero as he recognized the old man on his front steps as his father, whom he had not seen since he, his father, Howard Aaron Crosby, had come upon the family house in West Cove, Maine, one night after making rounds through the county selling brushes and soap to house-wives, seen his family in the dimly lit kitchen window, hit his mule, Prince Edward, with a hickory switch, and kept on down the road in his cart until he arrived, nameless, in Philadelphia.

His father sat on the edge of the couch with his hat in his lap and the motor of his rented car idling outside. Food steamed on the table and he said No, no, he couldn't stay. He asked how things were: Are you well? How are your sisters? Your mother? Joe? Oh, I see. And this is? Ah, Betsy. And you are? Claire, yes. Yes, yes, of course you are shy. I am a strange old man, yes. Well, no, I'd better be going. It was good to see you again, George. Yes, yes, I will. Good-bye.